OH MY CHILD

Virginia Aitken

Pen Press Publishers Ltd

Published in Great Britain by
Pen Press Publishers Ltd
25 Eastern Place
Brighton
BN2 1GJ

ISBN 978-1-906206-82-6

Printed and bound in Great Britain by
Cpod, Trowbridge, Wiltshire

A catalogue record of this book is available from
the British Library

Cover design by Jacqueline Abromeit

For Henry

CPP	CLN
CBA	CLO 9/08
CFU	CSR
CIN	CRE
CKI	CRI
CLE	CSA
CLH	CSH
CLHH	

Special Thanks to:

My husband, Henry Aitken,
for his support, interest, assistance, patient understanding,
collection of data, and proof-reading.

My mother, Audrey Goodwin,
for supplying me with many family stories and mementoes.

My daughter, Lynne Green,
for her interest and proof-reading.

My brother-in-law, John Aitken, and
my sister-in-law, Margaret Aitken,
for their helpful advice.

© Photo: Brian McKenna, Maghera

About the Author

Virginia Aitken was born in Preston, but now lives with her husband Henry in Magherafelt, a rural town set in the heart of Northern Ireland.

Having enjoyed a career as a teacher of English and Drama in grammar schools, she is now a freelance educational consultant and writer. She has written three novels, five educational books and has had her three plays performed on the amateur stage.

She and her husband, Henry, share the same hobbies of gardening, painting, and boating. They spend much of their holiday time travelling along the French waterways on their river cruiser, and are frequent visitors to the south of England, where all their grown up family live.

Novels by Virginia Aitken:

Oh My Child published in 2002 and 2008.
Snowdrops for Ada published in 2004.
Red Scar published in 2007.

Preface

Oh My Child is a biographical story in which some of the facts and events have been fictionalised. The story covers a seventy-year period during the nineteenth century and is set in and around the Isle of Ely in Cambridgeshire.

The facts and events in the novel have been gleaned from information found in wills, parish records, archive material, letters, diaries and stories in living memory. The thoughts, feelings and motivation of the real people in this story are based on the author's assumptions, deductions and conclusions drawn from that information.

The fictitious characters in the novel provide a colourful backdrop, and the people featured in the inauguration of Miss Pinkerton's Academy are all imaginary, and any similarity to persons living or dead is purely coincidental.

Chapter 1

February 2008

In my hand I hold an old visiting card with silver edges. On the one side in silver copperplate print is the name *Mrs Richard Porter* and on the other side, in faded black ink, is written a brief message:

> *My dear little girl.*
> *Oh my child, I shall soon have to leave you. And when this is given to you, you will be a big girl. This purse was given to my dear mother and now I give it to you.*

The few sad words on this little card have a story to tell, a story spanning seventy years, a story set in the heart of the Fens.

Chapter 2

RICHARD

February 1st 1822

The story begins in the heart of the Fens. Picture, if you will, a bleak, flat landscape on the eastern reaches of England, where man has waged his war against the relentless flooding of the farmland by the Great Ouse river and its many tributaries. It is a land of meres and drains. See the shored up rivers, whose gently rippling waters flow some thirty feet above the sombre, black-brown, peaty fields; whose levees and dykes are testament to years of communal labour. Look towards Ely, Queen Etheldreda's island, set in the midst of this once waterlogged landscape, and there you will see the cathedral, dominating the Cambridgeshire skyline. This "Ship of the Fens" rises majestically heavenward and touches the skies.

Come with me into this city, across Carmuckhill Bridge which spans the river. We can salute the cheery bargees below as they lead their towing horses to The Quay in the area they call "Babylon". We may even pause for a moment to consider the origins of this name: was it an isolated island of sorrowing exile, a place of refuge from the mediaeval tide of prejudice and persecution?

Let us now wander past *The Maltings*. Built in the nineteenth century, these premises were used for malting barley, a process of using high temperatures to cause cut barley to sprout. It was then sold to the many brewers in the city. We may look through the small window of a basket-maker's where the osiers are being closely woven into eel baskets. For the city of Ely was the Isle of Ely renowned for the eels caught there. We are enthralled as we walk through Ely's quaint streets, steeped in over a thousand years of recorded history. We may perhaps smile at the seeming humour of some of the names of the business premises: Chequer Lane is where we find Foster's Bank! and the High Street boot and shoemakers is called Legge and Son!

Suddenly we find ourselves in front of the cathedral, flanked by the fourteenth-century chapel and priory buildings. Somehow, close-up the impressiveness of "The Ship of the Fens" evaporates, as cattle surround us there on the green. The outer aspect is further diminished by the adjoining Bishop's Palace and the tall, two hundred-year-old plane tree in the palace garden. It is a cathedral to be seen from afar to fully appreciate its towering, exterior beauty.

So let me finally take you down St Mary's Street, and we shall stop here at St Mary's fourteenth-century church, as the strain of choristers echoes across St Mary's Green from the Chantry. For my story begins and ends right here. And it begins and ends with Richard.

The first February dawn of 1822 had cast a strange, watery light over this Cambridgeshire landscape, a hint of more sleet or perhaps some snow. Neither were welcome visitors, as man's tenuous hold over the fens could only become more fragile. Anxiety lined each farmer's brow as he wondered if his land would flood, if the levees would hold, but Richard was unaware of his own father's and his Uncle William's anxiety as their carriage rumbled through the cold towards Ely. He had his own anxieties.

He was six years old and frightened. This was the first time he had accompanied his father and his uncle William to the weekly Thursday market in Ely. In fact he had never before travelled outside the village of Haddenham where he was born. His mother Alice had filled him with the terrors which would befall any boy getting lost. Even now, he feared nothing more than to be lost and alone in Potter's Lane, a place where rough men lurked in the shadows, and even threw people into the dyke. As Richard tried to shake himself free of these untold terrors, his father was unwittingly fuelling his son's fears.

"I know it's hard to believe, William," he was saying to his brother. He nodded his head to affirm the truth of his words. "I am telling you it took three constables to restrain that ruffian. He'll hang, you know, before the year is out."

The word "hanging" brought more shivers to young Richard. He had never seen a public hanging, but he had heard about them often enough. Hadn't five of the Littleport rioters been hanged from specially constructed gallows at the Mill Pits in Ely? His mother and father and the older members of the family always spoke spiritedly about this particular form of execution, recollecting the festive atmosphere and the cheering, jeering crowds as a community rid itself of the wicked. Evil these men and women must surely be, Richard knew, but some inner voice of compassion whispered to him that hanging was wrong, that a human being's life was precious. Of course, he did not want to cross the path of a miscreant, but equally the barbarity of execution was instinctively abhorrent to him.

Uncle William was now shaking his head sadly, bemoaning the exodus of cottagers from Babylon, "It's lawlessness again, Henry. Decent folks on Babylon have to move out. Trapped they are. In the old days they could have walked across the waters to Ely on a plank or even have waded across, the water was that shallow."

Henry was thinking of days gone by when they were boys. "Do you remember how Farmer Ward would walk through the river to get to Ely? No more than thigh deep in those days."

"And if there was trouble, the constables could wade across to make arrests."

Such travel from Babylon would be impossible now. The river had been deepened, with large mounds of dredged silt deposited on the island. It was no longer a pleasant place to live, cut off from the rest of Ely, and from *The Ship Inn* where many a cottager would have enjoyed nightly jugs of the finest ale in Ely. Already a quarter of the local sheep farmers on Babylon had moved away. But, in their stead, foreigners were claiming these five cottages as their own.

"There's trouble enough now," intoned William. "They'll have to do something about the French." Wagging his finger, he sounded even more decisive, "Send them home is what I say."

Richard's anxieties took another direction now. Stories of French prisoners-of-war had been a regular topic of conversation ever since he could remember when his uncles came to visit on Sundays. He had listened to their tales of hard times during the war, but in the end how the mighty French leader, Napoleon, had been defeated at a place called Waterloo.

It was true that French soldiers had been kept captive in Ely during the war. On being released, most had made their way back to France to show support to the reinstated monarch, Louis XVIII. However, some were still in Ely, said to be "roaming free"; men who spoke a strange tongue; men who had killed; men who even wore the remnants of their uniforms; men who sharpened swords; men waiting to mass and fight their revolutionary cause again.

Sometime before, when he was very small, he had seen the Haddenham Volunteers in the smart red uniforms of the militia, as they marched down the street, past *Vine House* as he stood with his grandmother at the front door; he had waved and shouted with all the neighbouring children and their parents to support these brave soldiers wherever the noble English cause took them. He had been very proud that four of his very own relations had gone to fight against Napoleon, and even one of them had had a poem written about him beginning:

A gallant youth does then command,
Captain Porter, called by name, sir,
Who ready is to take the field,
If the French dare cross the main, sir.

But now the war was over, and Richard shuddered with the knowledge that the defeated French prisoners were roaming freely through the streets. What if one of them were to chase him and catch him and hang him for what the gallant youth, Captain Porter, had done all those years ago? Right now he wished that he was not a Porter; that he was back at home, warm and secure by the nursery fire with Jessie, the nurse-maid, and his younger brothers, Charles and Bill, or even in the drawing room with his mother.

This gave rise to his greatest anxiety this February morning, for he felt sorry for his cousin Marshall who had not been permitted to come with them. He was still only five. Richard and Marshall, with only three months separating them in age, were best friends: they played in the *Vine House* nursery together. Hardly a week went by when they did not visit one another. This morning when their carriage had pulled up outside Uncle William's farmhouse, Richard had been ever so excited at the prospect of sharing this day of days with his cousin. But instead, only Uncle William emerged from the front door. It was a blow, a miserable disappointment. Richard could keep quiet no longer.

"Where is Marshall?" he demanded. "I want him to come too!"

"Richard, you forget yourself. Forceful talk like that is very unbecoming in a young boy." His father was looking a little angry.

"Marshall is too young, Richard. You may count yourself lucky that your father is indulging you today. When we were boys, your grandfather only took us to Ely once we had reached the age of ten."

Henry was tense. He could have done without the kind of veiled criticism which his younger brother meted out regularly. It was especially unwelcome in front of the child. William, six years Henry's junior, was pugnacious by nature, never missing an opportunity to make a stand, to prove his superiority, even to come into direct conflict with his brother and vie for their parents' affection and support.

The most telling example of this was when William had suddenly and unexpectedly announced that he was to be married to Catherine Kefford on 21 February 1815. This was the very same day as Henry's forthcoming marriage to Alice Langford, for which preparations had been underway for many months. William had refused to change the date and Catherine preferred not to change the venue. As both weddings were to be held in different villages, the Porter family were inevitably divided. Consequently, Henry's marriage in Streatham, the village where Alice was raised, had been attended by his mother, his older sister Mary, his brother Charles, his aunt Ann and her family. William's marriage, by special licence, had taken place in Willingham, the village where Catherine was brought up, and had been attended by his father, his sister Ann, his Aunt Elizabeth and her family.

Unaware of his father's present thoughts, Richard felt chastened and cheated. Above all, he had wanted to share this day with his cousin. What fun they were to have had together! What an adventure it was to be! They had talked about it for weeks. As the carriage was drawing away, Richard looked through the small aperture in the side-door, and could distinctly see Marshall's flaxen curls and his tear-stained face at the upstairs window. That framed image of misery, frustration and envy was now gnawing away at him, adding to his sense of unease.

That early dawn journey from Haddenham to Ely to the artist's eye was one of ethereal beauty: stark windmills rose through the mists of the fens; the causeway which they travelled crossed the flat landscape like a ribbon. They passed through the village of Wilberton, across Streatham bridge, through Thetford and on towards Ely.

Richard had been glad that they had not taken the alternative route through Witchford to Ely. He had heard too many terrifying tales of evil which abounded there, so the gossips said, and also in nearby Witcham and Coveney. They were places of hanging, black cats and sorcery, where witches were burnt at the stake. Richard knew that his Uncle Charles and Aunt Mary lived in Coveney, and he nursed a secret fear that his Aunt Mary might be a witch, and would be hanged.

As the carriage approached the outskirts of Ely, it gathered speed once the hard, frosty tracks of the country roads had given way to the cobbles and square sets of Bugg's Hill, which led into St Mary's Street. Mr Stokes, the coachman, who proudly sported his thick, winter green livery worn on special occasions like today's visit to Ely, reined in the two dray horses, as the Bugg's Hill corner rapidly approached. By the time they had reached *The Eagle and Lamb* public house immediately before the corner on the right, they were travelling at a sedate pace.

"Fine premises there," said Richard's father, indicating the public house with its newly white-washed front and fine new tiled roof. "Good location too."

Richard was not too sure what was meant by the word "location", but he did assimilate the complimentary epithets. He liked the name of the public house, *The Eagle and Lamb*. He looked out at the colourful picture on the sign which was swinging and creaking in the chill, light wind. This depicted a curly-haired, innocent, white lamb and a fierce eagle standing side-by-side at the edge of a mountain crag, conjuring up a tale of adventure in young Richard's lively imagination.

Rounding the corner into St Mary's Street, abutting onto the pavement there was a large Tudor building with vertical oak-beam frontage, four chimneys, mullioned windows and a thatched roof.

"See that house, Richard?" Uncle William was pointing at this impressive two-storey building whose architecture set it apart from the Georgian designs of the rest of St Mary's Street.

"Yes, sir," replied Richard, looking obediently at the building indicated.

"Oliver Cromwell once lived there."

"Where does he live now?" Richard's knowledge of history did not go much further back than the Napoleonic Wars. Twenty or thirty years ago was history to a six-year old.

"Henry, do you teach this boy of yours nothing?" Richard was not sure whether he or his father was being admonished. One thing he was sure about, however, was that his father taught him much.

Henry sighed. William never lost an opportunity to prove himself.

"Oliver Cromwell is dead," Henry said, but before he could continue, Uncle William interjected.

"Information, Richard. Oliver Cromwell lived a hundred and fifty years ago… the first of the revolutionaries in Europe."

Oliver Cromwell, to him, was a man who had strong convictions and the courage to carry them out. It could be almost said that William tried to model himself on this most extraordinary figure in English history.

"An anti-Royalist!" snorted Henry, hoping to silence his brother.

"Mark my words! He was one of the greatest Englishmen ever to have lived."

"A would-be destroyer of our monarchy," argued Henry.

"A Fenman, through and through, Henry, as you well know."

"Only when it suited his purposes, as you well know."

It was a fact that Cromwell had supported the fenmen who feared that the king's plans to drain the fens would destroy their livelihoods. These fishermen had cheered their champion through the streets of Ely. Once Cromwell's Army, fired with Puritan zeal, had defeated the Royalists, and Cromwell himself had become the Lord Protector, he too came to appreciate that more taxes could be levied from drained lands as farm produce would increase ten-fold. This mercenary change of direction was difficult for Cromwell's ardent supporters to reconcile.

"He gave us a proper parliament," William countered, "the voice of the ordinary people."

"No, monarchy is all important. It maintains a nation's stability."

Now, as soon as Henry said this he knew that he was on slippery ground, for their present king, George IV, who had acted as Regent during his mad father's reign, was already proving to be a disastrous monarch: constantly at the centre of scandalous intrigues; frivolous in the extreme, spending the nation's money on architecture, interior decoration and fashion.

However, to Henry's relief, William was pressing his point home via another line of attack.

"Without him the fenlands would still be underwater," he said.

"He almost destroyed our heritage."

"The drained land is your heritage, Henry. Land is more important than all your high ideals. You should remember that."

Richard was not listening; he was a little bemused by the fact that his father and uncle were speaking so animatedly about someone who lived so long ago.

What he was listening to, however, was something entirely different, because by now they had stopped beside the green in front of St Mary's Church and the Chantry, where some thirty choristers were practising *Jesu Joy of*

Man's Desiring, in readiness for Sunday's worship. Canon Waddington, the choir-master, was renowned for his dedication to the glory of the Lord through magnificently rousing choral work. Richard was aware of a strange feeling, a faint tingling down his back. As the chill green shimmered in the lucent tones of the ever-lightening sky, with the last remnants of the night frost still clinging to the grass, and the blackbirds and sparrows silently fluttering this way and that in their desperate search for food, he suddenly knew that this quiet place held some special meaning for him.

He thought about the previous day, when Jessie, the nursery maid who was reading him the next instalment of *Treasure Island*, had suddenly shivered.

"Ooh, someone just walked over my grave," she had exclaimed, though how that could be so, Richard could not determine, seeing that she was sitting there, healthy and alive, in the nursery with him.

"What do you mean?" he had asked, a little bewildered.

"It's a premonition, like. A feeling you get when you know something bad is going to happen to you."

"What's going to happen to you?" He was now beginning to feel a bit fearful. Tears were not far away.

"Don't worry your pretty head," Jessie had said. "It's only an old wives' tale, I imagine." But she had not sounded convincing.

As Richard thought about all this, the scene before him imperceptibly altered. Was the ephemeral green shaded with a more sombre hue? He now noticed St Mary's graveyard beyond the green. He looked away, strangely disquieted.

Distant sounds of hooves and shouts of drovers permeated the stillness of the moment. Richard's contemplative mood was soon dispelled. The horses were coming. Thoughts were only fleeting after all: old wives and their tales were forgotten.

"Come on, my boy!"

His father, with an air of expectation about him, had bounded down from the carriage on to the pavement.

Mr Stokes lifted Richard down, patting him on the head, and said encouragingly,

"This'd be a wonderful day for you, Master Richard. There's nothing so grand as an 'orse fair. But mind you don't get trampled. Some of them 'orses is mighty heavy. Watch out for their feet!"

Leaving Mr Stokes to look after the 'orses and carriage, Richard, his father and his Uncle William walked purposefully to the far side of the green to await the arrival of the horses. Other buyers began to gather around the green too: gentlemen in search of a quiet mare for their wives; farmers to replace an aging plough-horse; successful tradesmen in need of additional cart-horses; eel trap and basket makers, whose livelihood depended on willows transported in donkey panniers; and brewers requiring powerful dray horses to transport their barrels of ale to the public houses which had ceased to brew their own. Many fenmen had travelled from as far away as Littleport and Soham, leaving at six in the morning. Richard was now surrounded by all these big people, and he held tightly to his father's hand, his mother's words of warning ringing in his ears.

Not only was his father excited, but there was also a heightening of expectation among the waiting crowd, which increased when the distant sound of hooves, clattering over the cobbles, could be heard.

"Here they come!" shouted a middle-aged farmer, as he peered up St Mary's Street up to Lamb Corner. The horses were coming from their temporary holding areas to the rear of the market in the centre of the town.

"Now, mind you stay close!" Henry told Richard.

Round the corner they came: an assortment of huge drays, shire horses, stud horses, Newmarket race-horses, sleek mares and fillies, hacks, ponies and donkeys. Richard caught glimpses of magnificent animals, whose nostrils breathed plumes of mist into the cold morning air

There was a cacophonous blend of drovers' whistles, double tongue-clicks, and cries of "Whoa there!", with the animals' whinnies, snorts and nickering. Richard was filled with wonder.

There must have been a hundred animals, of many different colours: white, dapple-grey, black, russet, piebald. Their drovers, assisted by the ostlers, stable lads and farmhands, firmly controlled them.

"Easy does it, my beauties," one drover was coaxing his two fillies into their designated roped area. He had positioned them to best advantage for a quick and profitable sale.

Henry jerked Richard by the hand as they followed Uncle William, who was now moving towards a group of shire horses: huge Suffolk Punches, soft brown with fringes of creamy hair over their hoofs. Their owner, Farmer Richard Bailey from Wilberton, had carefully roped them off from other horses for sale. There was something special about these animals. Uncle William was walking slowly round and round, inspecting, nodding, talking terms with Mr Bailey, exchanging money and making arrangements for the four horses to be delivered that day.

"Will you send one of your boys over today with them?" Uncle William asked, but his tone suggested that he would not be satisfied with that particular arrangement.

"I'll drive them there myself, Mr Porter," Richard Bailey offered.

Uncle William nodded. "Right."

"They're too valuable. Wouldn't trust anyone but myself to do the job," Farmer Bailey confided.

In actual fact, he was pleased to have completed such a quick sale. One half of his mind was saying that delivering them personally was an easy journey: just going back along the road he had come, after all. His farm in Wilberton was situated on the road to Haddenham. Delivering two of the carthorses to Henry Porter's malting business to the rear of *Vine House* on the main street of Haddenham and the other two to William Porter's farm at Hillrow on the other side of the village would be a simple matter.

The other half of his mind, however, suggested that had the Porters and the Baileys been more in contact with one another, then this whole journey to Ely horse fair and back could have been avoided. Time was precious. Richard Bailey was not prepared to waste any more of it. He would deliver the horses in person and get back to his ailing wife, Ruth.

Time was running out. Ruth was dying of consumption, and although he hoped against hope, he knew in his heart of hearts that she would not last the year. He thought about their two bonny daughters, Ann aged five and Margaret a year younger. How they were to fare without their mother was a nightmarish worry to the poor man. The thought of his life without Ruth in the years ahead was well-nigh unendurable.

"Don't tire them. Take them at an easy pace." Uncle William was an expert when it came to horses.

Business concluded, they made their way back to the carriage. Richard's head was still filled with the sights and sounds of the horse fair. But, gone were his anxieties. He felt exhilarated. He felt grown-up.

"Still in one piece, I see," said Mr Stokes, patting Richard's head once again. As he went to lift him into the carriage, Richard spoke decisively,

"I can manage on my own, thank you, Mr Stokes." He clambered aboard, but Mr Stokes ensured that, although he let young Richard manage unaided, a show of assistance was given for the benefit of Mr Henry Porter who might be watching.

Mr Stokes did not wish to incur the disapproval of his employer. He had a wife and five children, and times would be unbearably hard if he were to lose his job. Work was not easy to find these days, and already his two brothers had been forced to pull up their roots in Haddenham and search for employment elsewhere: Joshua far away in America to fruit farm, and John to the north of England as a collier. Yes, times were indeed hard, thought Mr Stokes, when decent folks had little alternative but to leave their families and travel to the other side of the world or to go down the mines. He would please Mr Porter, whatever it took.

Mr Stokes was still thinking of all this when there was an unfortunate occurrence. He pulled for all his life was worth on the horses' reins. Richard's heart was in his mouth as the carriage came to an abrupt halt; Uncle William was ejected from his seat, landing on his knees at Henry's feet, a lowly position which he was certainly not going to remain in for long; and Henry felt more than a little foolish and irritated, as his top hat teetered precariously on his head.

Richard thought his father and his uncle in their poses looked rather comic, like a cartoon he had once seen in an illustrated magazine. He wanted to smile, but just then his father sharply rapped with his brass-handled cane on the carriage roof.

His words reflected his mood, as he shouted through the misty pane of the communication hatch, "Stokes, what the devil is going on? Do you want to kill us all?"

"I'm sorry, sir. The Dean's wife got in the way."

"A lady, in the carriageway! Unthinkable! A pedestrian!" he retorted.

"No, Mr Porter, sir, she was in a Sedan chair."

Now whether a Sedan chair was classified as a vehicle or not would have been hard to decide by anyone in Ely at that time, as the Dean's wife was the only person to own one. Richard wondered why a lady would be sitting in the carriageway. He pictured the beautiful storyteller in *The Arabian Nights* as she sat for a thousand nights in the deserts of the Sudan, enthralling her captor, postponing her execution. It was not until a few years later when stories of colonial exploration of India were regular features in the *Ely*

Chronicle that young Richard came to understand that a Sedan chair had no connections with the Sudan.

"Drive on, Stokes!"

Henry had adjusted his hat and was looking at his brother brushing off the dust from his trim trousers. "No bones broken, William, I hope. You had quite a nasty fall there."

"Could have been much worse! He's a good man is Stokes. Quick-thinking! You're lucky to have him, Henry."

"And you, my boy, all in one piece?"

"Yes, Papa."

"Of course the boy is in one piece. If a boy can't take a little rough and tumble every now and again, then it's a sorry business."

The rest of the brief journey through the centre of Ely and to High Street was travelled in silence. There was no time, even at Lamb Corner, the city's crossroads, for Richard to take in the solidity of *The Lamb Hotel*, displaying its painted creamy façade which now proclaimed its new-found popularity. Since the opening of the turnpike roads, travellers from far and wide would stop overnight as the coach-horses were watered, fed and rested. *The Lamb Hotel* had flourished and prospered and the city was the better for it.

In no time they were at a standstill. The horses were secured on the hitching posts placed at three-yard intervals down the length of High Street, and Stokes was opening the carriage door.

"One hour, Stokes." Henry was busy interlocking his fingers to make his gloves feel snug and warm on his hands.

"Very good, sir." Stokes was blowing into his cupped hands. His body temperature was low. A big man, but even he was beginning to feel the cold.

"Conveniently positioned, I see. Right beside *The Bell*. Off you go and get a bowl of soup. Something to warm you."

Stokes smiled. His master was all right.

"You're too soft, Henry. Treat servants as they expect to be treated. You'll have trouble if you don't."

William knew all about servants.

Richard was hard-pressed to keep in step with his father and his uncle as they turned the corner into Market Place, no more than a narrow cobbled street whose overhanging buildings gave an impression of squalor and oppression. Richard did not like the slimy gullies. He did not like the uncertain shadows lurking in the doorways. Rounding the corner into Market Street, however, the ghosts and goblins evaporated. Here it was brighter, and his father was returning the greeting of the greengrocer whose shop occupied that corner site.

"Good morning, Mr Kempton, how is business?"

"Never been better," replied Mr Kempton. He grinned and spread his arms wide, though there were no customers near his shop.

"Good, good," was all that Henry could say.

Out of ear-shot, William shrugged his contempt for Mr Kempton. "How he keeps going at all is a mystery. The man never seems to try to get business. Why doesn't he close on market day? He must know by now that the people are at the stalls."

Henry liked Mr Kempton. He had kept his shop open through thick and thin, in all weathers, all through the wars against Napoleon when times were hard and agricultural produce scarce. Henry would not stand by, saying nothing, this time.

"Remember this, William. The family have been greengrocers there, on that very corner, since before your Oliver Cromwell was even born. Generations of them have made a living, through drought and flood, in times of war and in times of peace. I don't think the Kemptons deserve your censure."

Just as the surfacing tension between his father and uncle was beginning to disturb Richard, they rounded the old stonework corner. What a spectacle met Richard's young eyes! Ely Market! He knew that this was one of the oldest markets in the land, probably since the days of Queen Etheldreda, whenever that was, but right now he was not thinking about Ely history. He was overwhelmed by the hustle and bustle. It was true that itinerants came to Haddenham every so often to sell calico, wool dyes, snuff boxes and ladies' trinkets. There were even Frenchmen from Babylon, who came to sharpen scissors, scythes and household knives. But here, the Ely morning air was filled with the strident cries of forty or more marketeers who came from far and wide to sell their wares. The crowd jostled towards the colourful stalls, covered with their striped canopies. They were here to snap up bargains.

The stall-holders' cries rang out: "highly desirable, sir" and "the cheapest you're going to find in the land, I tell you ma'am" and "going for a song, my dear." The townsfolk with money to spend never failed to be gullible.

A large crowd had gathered near the butter market. Richard strained to see what all the commotion was about.

"Papa, what's happening over there? May we see?"

William had known that it would not be propitious to bring youngsters to the market. He would not let Marshall accompany him until he was at least nine years old. Why Henry should wish to be burdened with a child at Ely market was beyond his comprehension. He turned to his brother, a look of exasperation creeping across his square face.

"Henry, I'll go and strike the deal with Jim Timson," he said, turning towards the poultry market. Then with a brush of his hand, he added, "You take the boy to see Madame Zorra."

The dismissive, yet patronising tone did not go unnoticed.

"Tell him we'll take nothing less than the same standard as the last batch. Nothing less." Henry tried hard to rally, to sound forthright, a man who knew what he wanted. In reality Henry did not know much about geese, and William did.

William was an expert on geese too.

Madame Zorra! That was a name to excite a young boy, especially a boy with a passion for adventure stories, and heroes with names to fire the imagination: Man Friday, Blind Pew, Icarus and now Madame Zorra. There she stood, resplendent in gypsy apparel. Her red skirt was embroidered with strange hieroglyphic designs in gold thread and hemmed with tassels which barely covered her ankles. Richard's mother would not have approved. A low-cut white camisole interlaced with crimson ribbon only partially covered her gently rising bosom. Richard was transfixed. He wanted to reach out and stroke the smooth, white skin, and lay his head against her soft, rounded breasts. Somehow, he knew his mother would have ushered him away.

Madame Zorra wore a black silken shawl, edged with a myriad of twinkling, glass beads. Some onlookers might have said it had accidentally slipped off her left shoulder, but other more worldly members of the male audience knew that it was deliberate: this voluptuous, young woman had learnt the art of seduction from her mother even before she could talk. On her head she wore a mauve scarf tied tightly round the crown, barely restraining her wild, black, curled tresses. Matching, gaudy, brass rings dangled from each ear, and thirty bracelets jangled on each arm.

Madame Zorra was a fortune-teller, who would come to the three-day fairs in May and October, but never before had she been to the weekly market. She must have fallen on hard times to be here in Ely on a cold day in February. But she knew the crowds would gather round in this city of long traditions, just as they had gathered round her mother and her grandmother before.

"I see in your life a young, handsome man." Her high-pitched voice, with its faintly foreign accent sounded mysterious. The likely lass whose palm she held giggled and grew pink, for her beau, Thomas Gotobed, stood close by. The crowd laughed as a local lad held a pointed finger above

Thomas's head for all to see who the "young, handsome man" was.

"I see a long life ahead with many healthy children." There was more laughter and someone clapped the young man on the back, amid shouts from the crowd:

"She'll keep you busy, Thomas!"

"When are the banns, eh?"

Poor Thomas! He was at once embarrassed and proud. He did not know where to look. He ran forward and grabbed his sweetheart's hand and away they fled.

"Papa, can she really see what is going to happen?"

"The folks hereabouts think she can, son."

Richard took his free hand out of his pocket and looked at his palm, but could see nothing but a criss-cross of pink lines. He saw no future there at all.

Madame Zorra had already been paid her farthing and she was secretly eager to move on to another hopeful with a copper coin at the ready.

But she looked down at the child before her who examined his palm so seriously.

"Tell him his future, then," old Simon Stead, his clay pipe clamped between his few remaining teeth, called out. "He's a young'n. You couldn't go far wrong wi' him." He wheezed his amusement to his cronies. "He's plenty of life in him to see!"

There were a few guffaws. Madame Zorra felt her credibility beginning to slip away. She knelt down to the youngster, reached forward and gently took the cold, little, upturned hand between her ringed fingers. The boy's father inclined his head to give his assent.

"I see a long life. Wives and children."

The crowd were still restless. This could be anyone's future! Madame Zorra looked hard at the child and deep into the vaguely troubled, yet kind eyes of his father.

"I see family divisions."

Then she traced one long, curved line on Richard's palm. What she saw there was unusual and rarely seen. Her eyes took on a dreamy, far-away expression, as she looked straight into Richard's eyes. He, unblinking and strangely sleepy, was spell-bound. It was a special moment, timeless, yet caught in time.

"I see a full circle."

"Ooh, it's a full circle," whispered a buxom bystander to her elderly mother, who had been straining to hear the fortune-teller's every word.

Like Chinese whispers the crowd passed this enigmatic piece of destiny knowingly from one to the other, though what it was they knew would have been difficult to ascertain.

Richard's anxiety began to return. He pulled his hand away. Perhaps evil was to befall him after all, for hadn't his mother warned him. He grabbed his father's hand and held it tightly, urging his father away, away from Madame Zorra. The spell was broken.

The direction they took was down through the thronging market towards the far end. There stood an impressive, old building, with bars on the windows.

"That's the Bridewell, Richard. Take note, eh!"

"Yes, papa!" he said, but was not sure what he was to take note of. "Is that where people get married?" It seemed a reasonable question.

Henry looked strangely at him. "Married! That's the gaol!" A rueful expression crept across his face. He thought about his wife.

Richard knew now why he must take note. That must be the very gaol where the Littleport rioters were kept before they were hanged. He knew all about them. He wanted to go home. His thoughts were interrupted by Uncle William.

"That's all settled. Timson himself will bring the geese tomorrow. He'll come to me first, naturally, seeing he's coming from Earith direction. You'll need to have your pen ready by midday."

Jacob and Moses, twin brothers who had been farm-hands to the Porter family since the days of Richard's grandfather, had erected the geese enclosures in readiness. Richard had been there as his father gave instructions and supervised the men. He knew the pens were ready. He wondered why his father sighed, yet said nothing.

"Uncle William," he ventured, "the pens are ready now. Papa and I made sure."

But his uncle was not listening.

"Now, I'll go and send Stokes over to Tattersalls. Any objection, Henry, to using your man?" He did not wait for an answer. "He can see to Catherine's order for the infant. He'll be passing Tallow Lane, so he can get a couple of boxes of candles too."

Henry was looking affectionately at his son who had spoken up for him. What a fine boy he was! He determined there and then to treat him to something special.

Uncle William marched ahead.

"You'll find us in Legge's," Henry called after his brother.

And that was how Richard was the first Haddenham boy under nine years of age to have his very own riding boots. Uncle William tutted and shook his head sadly as Mr Legge measured Richard's feet, continually admonishing his brother for spoiling the boy. He was not going to buy his son riding boots before the age of twelve.

On the way home they opened the pannier containing a lunch specially prepared by Mrs Vinney, the *Vine House* cook. Inside was what she believed to be "good wholesome food to sustain the travellers": freshly baked bread, ham, apples, ale and milk. In normal circumstances, Henry and his brother would like to have lunched at *The Lamb Hotel*, for it was well-known for such culinary delights as duckling, Cottenham cheeses, asparagus and eels, but William had not wished to be away too long, as his wife was getting close to her time: only a couple of weeks before the birth of their third child.

No sooner had their carriage drawn up outside William's farm in Hillrow than Hilda the maid came rushing out, her skirts flying, her cap awry.

"It's the mistress," she exclaimed. "She's took bad!" She puffed and panted as she spoke.

"For God's sake, woman, what's happened?" Uncle William grew pale, fearing the worst.

"The doctor is with her now. It's the child! It's coming! But, sir, feet first, sir."

What agonies William suffered! "Dead! Do you mean dead?"

"Oh Lord bless you, sir, no! It's the wrong way round, sir. It's alive and kicking, all right. As I say, sir, feet first." Tittering at her small joke, Hilda once more picked up her skirts and disappeared into the house.

William had not expected his wife's confinement for at least another fortnight. He was miserable and frustrated that he should have been away from home at this time. He was sick with worry. Catherine was the very centre of his being.

Richard watched now how calmly his father took charge of the situation.

"Look, Catherine's a strong woman. She's given birth already to two healthy sons with no trouble."

He now had his arm round his brother's shoulder, gently assuring him that all would be well.

"You know Doctor Grainger is competent and highly respected, William. Let us go inside and wait downstairs for news. I think a brandy would be in order."

As they entered the house, William was much more composed. Henry, concerned for his young nephew, turned saying,

"Come, Richard, you must go and find Marshall. He'll be in the nursery helping to look after Stephen, I imagine. I think he would appreciate your company right now."

Richard felt good inside. The image of his cousin's face at the window had haunted him throughout the day, and now he was able to do something to help make things better. He had also seen the real Henry at last, no longer the man who bore the brunt of a younger brother's seemingly superior personality, but a man who acted calmly and decisively in a crisis, a man who showed concern and sympathy for those in need. Richard was filled with pride for the man who was his father.

Chapter 3

RICHARD

Christmas 1832

Once upon a time, before Sir Cornelius Vermuyden had unleashed his genius upon this corner of England, the village of Haddenham, at little more than a hundred feet above sea-level, had been an island in a virtual fenland sea. Since the times of the Vikings and the Romans, this low-land of Norfolk and Cambridgeshire was constantly inundated: from the south by the peaty, seeping waters of the Great Ouse river as it overflowed its banks; and from the north by the angry spring-tide seawater which broke through the ancient and crumbling breakwaters at Lynn.

During the seventeenth century, this great Dutch engineer, Vermuyden, envisaged a vast network of dykes and drains discharging water into natural rivers and outfalls. Where once there had been meres and marshes, crops would grow in their plenty. Supported by staunch foreign "Gentlemen Adventurers", mainly Huguenots and Walloons fleeing from Roman Catholic oppression in France and Belgium, he devised a plan to drain the Fens. This was a mammoth project, partly funded by these dispossessed Protestants.

If you stand on North Hill, which is the highest point of Haddenham, and look towards Earith in the west, you can make out in the distance the straight outline of the Hundred Foot Drain, named the Bedford Drain after an English benefactor. It is a long raised channel, which takes water thirty miles in a straight line from the Fens to the Great Ouse near Lynn. Take a moment to look northwards across North

Fen towards the village of Sutton, and all around you can make out the hap-hazard network of "cuts", drains which cross the depressed landscape like giant cicatrices.

Turning your head slightly in the direction of the low winter afternoon sun, you may shade your eyes as you watch a few tradesmen on the causeway out at Hillrow bringing their wares from Earith to Haddenham. Beyond this raised road lies the rich farmland of Gall Fen and Adventurers' Fen where the Great Windmill and Neville's windmill stand still on this windless day.

"There's not enough wind for the two on 'em!" was what Farmer Sears always said on these calm, winter days. Perhaps he was right.

Beside the village pond on the green in the centre of the village, a knot of carters talk animatedly together as they oversee the washing of their carthorses' hooves. We make our way past them up to the crossroads, where the old finger signpost points us down Main Street in the direction of Wentworth and Ely.

As we walk down this street, there on the left, set in the midst of an ancient graveyard, and protected by a copse of gnarled, old oaks, stands the fourteenth-century Holy Trinity Church, whose lofty steeple houses the five great bells which can be seen for miles. It is said that Ovin, Queen Etheldreda's steward brought Christianity to Haddenham in the seventh century. Certainly the base of a Saxon cross was found in Haddenham in 1770 with the inscription "O God grant Thy light and rest to Ovin, Amen", and it is firmly believed by the excited people of Haddenham to be a monument to this monk of antiquity.

Continuing on our way down Main Street, you can look between the doctor's house and the blacksmith's shop on the right, across to Hinton Hall, the stately home where Lord Hardwicke resides. Beyond his estate, we can scan the rich brown colours of Grunty Fen and gaze towards Ely, where the ecclesiastical "Ship of the Fens" dominates the north-eastern skyline.

Straight ahead of us, at the bottom of the gently sloping hill there we can just make out one of the two clay pits of the village, the one where yellow clay is dredged and used in the Porter family's brick-making business. Witchford village stands on a distant ridge four miles away, and beyond that the village of Coveney lies, at the heart of acres of rich, agricultural land.

We find ourselves standing outside a fine timber-frame house with steps leading up to a large, oak, panelled door. This is *Vine House*, with *The Maltings* to the rear. The property was built during the restoration period in 1665 by Clement Porter, who, like his father and grandfather before him, had been the village maltster.

Vine House has been the Porter family home for generations, passing from eldest son to eldest son. This is where Richard was born. *Vine House* would be his one day.

The silence in *Vine House*, on Christmas dawn of 1832 was both eerie and exciting for little Suzanna, as she tiptoed barefoot along the polished wooden floor of the upper corridor towards her brother's room.

She had woken too early on this special day of celebration and feasting. All the rest of the Porter family were asleep. It was very cold in the bedroom under the eaves which she shared with her nine-year old sister. The fire which had burned so brightly in the bedroom grate on Christmas Eve, when she had been put to bed by Jessie, had gone out, with not even a dying ember to take the chill off the air.

Suzanna had sensed a strangeness in the world. Lying there in the darkness, she had become aware of a bluish light filtering through the chink in the red velvet window drapes. Then she had heard an uncanny, muffled stillness outside, as if all sound had been muted. She climbed onto the blanket chest with its carefully worked tapestry cushion cover, and peeped out through the misted glass of the latticed bedroom window. The magical world she saw in the street outside filled her young heart with a delight which she wanted to share.

Her older sister Ann lay sleeping soundly in the double bed, which the two of them shared. Suzanna knew that she would not waken Ann, for Ann would spoil the magic. Just the previous morning, she had heard a scratching noise in the eaves. Thinking there might be long-tailed rats trying to get in, she had been scared and prodded her sister awake. Even though it really was near the time to waken, when there was light in the sky, when the servants below were already stirring, Ann had shouted crossly at her,

"I've told you and told you. Don't waken me. My dreams are not to be broken midway." She had pulled the coverlet over her, neither offering comfort nor allaying her five-year-old sister's fears.

Suzanna reached up to lift the latch of the bedroom door, taking care not to make a sound. Not wishing to waken her parents either, she had avoided the creaking boards outside their bedroom. She knew that, although her father would only gently admonish her and carry her back to bed, her mother would speak severely to her and send her back to her room.

In her mind she could hear her mother's words, "I have warned you before. Disturb the household early and you will go to bed early, with no supper. It's as simple as that." Today of all days, she did not want to go to bed early. But she had to tell someone about the winter wonderland she had seen outside.

Richard was her favourite brother. As the eldest of the three brothers, he always had time for her and she loved him unreservedly. So she made her way past the bedroom shared by Charles and Bill, down the two steps at the head of the dark stairwell, and felt her way along the dim, narrow passage towards Richard's room which nestled cosily under the eaves at the other end of the house.

"Wake up! Wake up! Oh, Richard, please wake up!" Suzanna stood by his bed and blew on his brow and ruffled his dark brown, wavy hair.

Richard woke with a start. Was there light in the sky? Had he over-slept? Someone was pulling back the bed-clothes, now tugging at the sleeve of his night-shirt.

"Get up, Richard! Come and see!" the high-pitched tones of his sister's voice finally penetrated Richard's consciousness. It was Christmas-time. Moreover, it was night-time.

At sixteen, on one of the few mornings of the year when he was able to indulge himself by sleeping more than his customary seven hours, Richard could have done without the dawn antics of his five-year-old sister. There was no doubt that he loved his little sister, but why did she have to come and plague him this Yuletide morning? There was no sign of light in the sky yet! Surely she could play with Ann! After all they were more of an age, with only four years between them. Ann could read her stories and keep her amused.

This was his well-earned holiday. Go away! Go back to your room! is what he wanted to say.

"Oh, don't tell me to go away!" Suzanna's pink lips quivered and her grey eyes looked watery. "You're the only one awake."

Two years of farming and working in the brewery had begun to make a man of Richard and he wanted to shoo his sister away, but the brother in Richard, that kind and patient person whom she adored, could not find it in his heart to send her away. So there he was, being led like a sleep-walker to the window, and a little, excited voice beside him was piping.

"Look, Richard. It's all white with snow."

They stood hand in hand at the window together, Suzanna's tiny freezing fingers wrapped in Richard's strong warm grasp. Both were mesmerised by the virginal blanket of the snow which they beheld on that cold, hushed morning when the rest of the world was asleep.

"A white Christmas!" Richard shared the magic of the scene before them with his young sister, but a chill touched his heart too. He was filled with memories of another Christmas, six years earlier, when snow had fallen during the night. The house had been in mourning for his baby brother, Henry, who had died of croup a week before Christmas. He had not even reached his second birthday. There had been no celebrations that year. The ten-year-old Richard had taken on the role of comforter to his two younger brothers, while his parents grieved apart. The snow brought neither joy nor comfort then: it was a cold and cheerless blanket which lay over the little grave in Holy Trinity churchyard.

Richard suddenly felt cold.

Suzanna looked up at him. "It's like magic," she whispered, with a sweetly curving smile on her lips, and her eyes twinkled like the glistening snow outside.

"Come on. Into bed. Let's get warm," he said, casting the sad memories to the back of his mind. "It's cold out here."

Together they slipped under the covers of his bed, pulling them right up over their bodies until only two heads could be discerned in the magical darkness. She snuggled up beside him, her cold knees touching his stomach and her icy toes tucked under his thighs. Together they waited for the rest of the house to stir. Richard closed his eyes.

"Richard."

Her voice was bewitching, and she knew it.

"Yes."

"Tell me a story."

The rising intonation was hard to refuse, and he knew it.

"Go to sleep!"

"Please."

His heart melted. "Very well," he sighed. "Now, don't wriggle. Lie as still and as quiet as a mouse. Are you ready?"

"Yes."

"Once upon a time, there was a brave Saxon warrior called Owadin. He lived right here in The Fens in a time before they were drained. There was water all around in those days. It was a sight to behold. Owadin was the champion of The Fens."

"What's a champion?"

"He was the best at fighting. Owadin was the very best. He was the champion. One day, he was leading his band of warriors across Adventurers' Fen, moving swiftly with the wind on his face. They were no ordinary warriors, for they did not go on horseback. Oh no, not they! They walked on stilts, ten feet long, across the marshy land, to meet the enemy.

"And the enemy came from far away, from a land across the sea. These men were Danes who came to steal Owadin's land, where he fished for eels. The Danes came in their long boats, with their oars and their spears. They spoke a different language and they looked fearsome with their flowing, yellow hair and their horned helmets.

"But Owadin and his men were not afraid. For they knew that the Danish ships would be stuck in the shallow waters of Adventurers' Fen. And so it was. The ships were caught fast in the sucking gault. No matter how hard they tried, the Danes could not get their boats out of that sticky red clay at the bottom of the fen.

"Owadin shouted, 'Forward, men!'

"And his men attacked on their high stilts, striding through the marshy, peaty waters of the fens. The enemy looked up at these giants and were afraid. They tried to flee, swimming and thrashing about in the water. Not a man of them got away. And that is how Owadin saved The Fens from the enemy. That is why he is called the 'Champion of The Fens'."

As the sky lightened, the dawning day promised to be clear and bright. The orange sun just above the horizon cast long blue-grey shadows across the pink hues of the snow, which lay in all its pristine glory across the distant landscape.

Suzanna lay peacefully asleep. Richard too had been dozing, wakening now to the sounds of activity in the kitchen, which was situated directly underneath his bedroom.

In her basement quarters, a comfortably furnished room with a fire and all that a middle-aged woman could reasonably want, Mrs Vinney was generally the first to waken. She had always been a light-sleeper, one of those rare individuals who only need five hours sleep each night. It never seemed to do her harm, for a more robust woman would be hard to imagine. In appearance, as well-rounded as she was well-fed, her voluminous cook's clothing and pinafore apron only added to the overall largeness of her person.

Now she was bustling about, getting the final preparations for the Christmas feast under way. This was the day of the year when she could exercise her culinary skills to the full. The two geese selected for this festive fare had been hung for a full ten days. They were from a batch of good quality birds supplied as always by Jim Timson. The puddings had been prepared in the autumn when the plums had been ripe. They had been maturing in their muslin pouches down in the cellar. Mrs Vinney had every item on the menu under control, and she got to work with noisy enthusiasm.

By contrast, the stable yard was still and quiet. However, Mr Stokes would soon arrive, in his special green livery, to get the horses and carriage ready to take the family the short distance to Holy Trinity Church for Christmas morning service.

Richard now stood at his bedroom window and looked out. The snow on the lower rooftop of their adjoining brewery was decorated with a delicate pattern of birds' filigree footprints.

Mrs Vinney would throw some crumbs out for the birds, he was certain, as she went about her business in the kitchen.

Richard could hear her voice now, "Christmas comes but once a year, and when it comes it brings good cheer. So, Clara, be cheerful!"

Clara was the new scullery maid. She was only fourteen years old and Mrs Vinney was always reminding her that she was fortunate to be in employment in *Vine House*. Even now she was continuing in the same vein,

"Mark my words, working here will help you move upwards. You want to be in a better situation, don't you, girl? Assistant cook is what you'd like, isn't it? Or maybe you could even train to be a housekeeper. Wouldn't that suit you nicely?"

Normally Clara would have agreed with Mrs Vinney, for she was indeed determined to secure a more prestigious situation before she reached the age of sixteen, although she was realistic enough to know that to be housekeeper might be beyond her reach, unless fortune were to smile on her. But today was Christmas Day and she longed to be at home with her four younger brothers, enjoying the fun and games around the peat fire in the family's cosy tithe cottage out at Hillrow. Instead she had woken in the basement room which she shared with Louisa. Although she would admit that it was comfortable and afforded her much more room and amenities than those which she was used to, it still was not her home.

Louisa was the parlour maid and the chamber-maid. It was she who tended to the eight fires in the house, and brought pitchers of hot and cold water to all the bedrooms every morning. Louisa was a lusty girl of sixteen, who secretly adored Mr Richard. She looked forward each day to entering his bedroom to place the water pitchers on the dresser and make up the fire. She would secretly look at him from under her dark lashes, breathe in deeply as she ran her eyes over his sleeping form, and lick her lips as she let her imagination wander.

When Louisa came into Richard's room this Christmas Day, her heart leapt, for there he was standing at the window, with his back to her. He was in his nightshirt, his muscular body beneath silhouetted against the glow in the eastern sky. In her agitation, she spilled some water from the hot water jug over her foot. She let out a shriek. The moment was shattered. Richard started and turned round to see what was happening; Suzanna awoke with a gasp; poor Louisa felt totally humiliated in front of her adored young master.

"Is it Christmas? Is it Christmas?" Suzanna was clapping her hands excitedly.

"No harm done, Louisa?" Richard was asking, "I hope you are not scalded."

"No, sir," Louisa mumbled miserably.

"Yes, it's Christmas now," Richard answered his young sister who was jumping up and down on his bed. "Happy Christmas, my dearest!"

Worse and worse for Louisa! How Louisa wished that she, and she alone, were his "dearest". She looked down at the floor, her head hung down, her shoulders heaving with an involuntary sob. It was all too much to bear.

"Come, come, Louisa," Richard was now concerned. "I fear you are scalded. Let's get you down to Mrs Vinney. She will be able to dress it with some beeswax and gauze." He ushered her through the door. "Suzanna, stop that bouncing! You'll break the springs! You may go and knock on Jessie's door, though she'll be awake now with all the commotion, no doubt, eh Louisa?" He had meant it kindly, but Louisa looked more and more uncomfortable at having been the cause of the "commotion" and perhaps having incurred Mr Richard's displeasure. But he was smiling at her.

"Happy Christmas, Louisa," he said to her, in the narrow corridor leading to the back stairs. It had been said to her, and to her alone. She was cheered. "Happy Christmas, sir."

The Christmas peal of bells echoed through the village, as each of the five bell-ringers pulled on his stout rope in Holy Trinity church tower. They had begun with fifty rounds, the individual bells repeatedly ringing out from highest to lowest. They finished with a joyous series of sixty carefully practised changes, a symphony of music created by ringing the bells in special, learned sequences.

"There's nothing like the sound of bells on Christmas morning!" Mrs Vinney was telling young Clara. "It's never quite the same for evensong." Mrs Vinney sighed. She would have preferred to attend morning service, but the servants generally attended evening service, after the festivities of the day were over. She had to prepare a Christmas lunch for twenty-two people and there was much to be attended to.

The chief campanologist was proud of his team of bell-ringers: they had mastered exactly half of the changes possible with five bells, and had only taken a year to perfect them. He was determined that in the following year of 1833 they would master the second half.

The two Porter families sat in their pews at the front of the congregation. In the front row sat Richard's grandparents, Henry and Mary, now in their seventies. They no longer lived in *Vine House* with their eldest son and his family. They had moved into more modest accommodation specially built on the land adjoining *Vine House*. There they enjoyed relative peace and quiet, away from the daily comings and goings of Henry and Alice's family, yet, were able to stay close to keep in touch.

In days gone by, Henry and Mary had sat with their children in this front pew, hopeful that it would always be so. They were always saddened when Christmas came around, for it highlighted the fact that their family was scattered, with only Henry and William remaining in Haddenham. Henry, as the eldest, sat in this front pew with them, along with his wife and family. Jessie was there too, tucked in beside Suzanna at the end of the row.

On the second pew sat William and his family, with Hilda the nursemaid tending to Mary and Rachel, the two youngest. Catherine rarely attended church: she had chosen not to be married in a church. Life had been more than kind to her; she had no need to pray for guidance or for strength to overcome adversity. Giving thanks for her honeyed existence and bounty never occurred to her. When William ventured out on the occasional Sunday, he would attend evensong and sit in the front pew. He did not take kindly to the indignity suffered as a younger brother on occasions such as today's family outing, and fully envied his two other brothers Charles and Robert, also younger than Henry, who were able to avoid similar indignity, by marrying into rich farming families in Coveney.

The vicar's Christmas message focused on the tragedy of the two unfortunate ladies who had perished the previous week when the high-sided stage-coach, in which they had been travelling from Earith to Cambridge, had overturned and crashed into Hillrow Fen. There had been much discussion about the dangers of stage-coach travel of late; the majority of coach drivers were too proud of the traditions of their coaching heritage to accept the innovative "safety" coach.

"We pray for their souls, and spend a few moments in silent thought as we consider their grieving families not many miles away in Earith. We must thank all those in the congregation who gave of their unstinting assistance, and share their pain that their efforts were in vain."

When the service was over, the Porter family filed reverently down the aisle, past the rest of the congregation. Richard saw all the familiar faces: all the Granger family sat at the front on the other side of the aisle. Like Henry and William Porter, they too were wealthy farmers in the Haddenham area. Richard nodded to some of his friends from his days at Arkenstall School for Boys. There was Mr Palmer, the butcher and his strapping family. The Setchells, the Suttons and the Rose family sat across the aisle from Mr and Mrs Metcalfe from *The Plough Inn*.

Near the back was Clement Porter, the shoemaker, with his wife, Sarah. Although theirs was a completely different Porter family, Sarah would often bask in reflected glory as she gossiped with her neighbours.

"My dears," she would say with a patronising incline of the head, "Only the other day I was saying to Alice..." dropping a hint that, by being on first name terms, she and her husband must be related to the *Vine House* Porters.

Just as Richard was considering the sameness of every Christmas, there in the semi-darkness at the back of the church stood Mr Bailey, who was not a regular parishioner. Although Mr Bailey himself was well known in the village, his daughters were not. Ann, now aged 15, and Margaret aged 14, had seldom been to Haddenham. None of them had been to Holy Trinity before. Mr Bailey had been pressurised by his two daughters to attend Holy Trinity Christmas service this year, rather than attend Wilberton Parish Church as they usually did. There were two reasons for this: the first was that Christmas always made their father sad. Memories of his wife Ruth were too painful. Although she had been dead for nine years, standing before her grave each Christmas under the single yew tree in Wilberton churchyard, brought acute memories of her thin, skeletal body in her final trial. His girls wanted him to try to forget. The second reason was that they were secretly hoping to catch a glimpse of the Porter boys and hoping that the Porter boys would notice them!

Richard looked at the taller of the two girls and caught his breath. In the church candlelight, the chestnut curls of her hair shone richly as they cascaded over her shoulders from under her pale blue bonnet. The beauty of her face, and her natural grace overpowered him. He smiled. She smiled.

He walked in a daze past the font with its carved griffins, the title of the closing hymn, *Light Shining out of Darkness*, taking on a whole new meaning for him. This hymn by William Cowper had always appealed to him, but never till now did he fully appreciate the import of the words.

God moves in a mysterious way,
His wonders to perform.
He plants his footsteps in the sea,
And rides upon the storm.
Deep in unfathomable mines
Of never failing skill,
He treasures up his bright designs,
And works his sovereign will.

As Richard shook hands with the vicar, his mind was filled with the firm belief that God had indeed performed *wonders*. There was no doubt that this day was one of God's *bright designs*, and that *His sovereign will* was that he should marry Mr Bailey's older daughter. He asked the vicar the names of the daughters, casually, so as not to arouse curiosity.

"The older girl, the one with the chestnut curls, is Ann. Fifteen she is. An accomplished pianoforte player I understand. She virtually runs the Bailey household. Mrs Bailey died some years ago, you know."

Richard did not know much about the Baileys except that Mr Bailey had a successful studfarm and reared horses.

"A sad case. A sad case." The vicar tutted and went on, "The younger girl is Margaret. She's a practical girl by all accounts; will make an excellent farmer's wife, some day."

Outside the church, Ann and Margaret were hurried to their waiting carriage, pulled by two magnificent Suffolk Punches, for Mr Bailey never lost an opportunity to advertise. Richard caught a glimpse of a delicate ankle in the folds of the flounce at the bottom of Ann's skirt as she was whisked up into the carriage. He looked as daringly as he could without arousing suspicion at her face: her beautiful features; her porcelain skin; her high cheekbones; her finely tapering eyebrows; her shining, smiling blue eyes; her inviting, wetted lips; and her crowning glory of richly coloured curls.

Alice meanwhile was supervising Mr Stokes as he deposited gifts into the boxes set in the porch. These gifts were mainly foodstuffs to be distributed amongst the poor the following day. This ancient Boxing Day tradition had not died out in Haddenham. Christmas was a time for remembering the needy and less fortunate. Just four days earlier, on Goodening Day, widows of the village had called, by tradition, at the larger houses for a little something for Christmas. Alice Porter, a good woman at heart, though often perceived as indomitable and stern, usually had packets of tea and some money ready for these expected visitors. As tea was hard to come by, and was expensive, Alice knew this was a most welcome gift.

She looked over at her eldest son, who was staring after the Baileys' departing carriage. She noted the expression on his face. How like his father he looked at that moment! Like Henry had looked when she first married him. There was a sudden rush of blood to her face as she thought of love-making. She tried so hard to be upright and independent, keeping control of her husband and putting her sexual desires to the back of her mind. She did not always succeed, however, and she and Henry enjoyed what was in fact a relatively secure and happy marriage.

Yes, at times, Henry felt trapped and inferior to his wife, who managed the large, ever-expanding brewery with commercial acumen. She ruled the thirty employees with organisational expertise and an iron fist. But he did love his wife, and his physical desires for her were as strong now as they were on their wedding day.

Richard was suffering from what he knew must surely be "love at first sight". A long time ago, Jessie had told him all about her husband, Bert, who had gone to war against Napoleon and had perished at sea in the Battle of Trafalgar. It was a sad tale, but Jessie's fond memories kept her cheerful and buoyant, when many another widow succumbed to inarticulate grief.

"Let me tell you," she had confided to Richard, "it was love at first sight."

"What's love at first sight?" he had innocently asked. He was seven at the time.

"He was that handsome in his sailor suit. And when I clapped eyes on him, my heart was all a flutter, and I was quite breathless. That's love at first sight."

"You loved him before you talked to him?" Richard had sounded incredulous.

"That's right, dearie. And do you know what, he fell in love with me straight too." To dispel any inklings of doubt in her young listener's mind, she had added, "I was quite attractive in those days. We made a bonny couple, my mother said."

Richard knew that he had fallen in love, at first sight. He also knew that he and Ann Bailey would make a "bonny couple". He knew, without a shadow of a doubt that Ann Bailey would one day change her name to Mrs Ann Porter. What a happy day that would be! He would work hard at the future career already set in motion for him in *The Maltings*. He would be a fine maltster like his father and grandfather before him; he would brew the finest beer; and what's more he would try hard to succeed in farming some of the land his father had acquired at the time of the Enclosure Acts. He would work hard to become a worthy husband.

Normally he and Marshall would have bounded into the house to pester Mrs Vinney, noisily and dramatically sniffing the air which was filled with delicious aromas of cooking, cheekily poking their fingers into the cranberry sauce, and begging to know when the Christmas lunch would be ready.

"Bless me!" she would say. "It'll take twice as long with you young men scampering about in my kitchen." And with a flurry of her apron, she would chase the boys out of the way.

40

Today Richard was more subdued and pensive. Marshall was accompanied instead by his cousin Charles, in what he regarded as his right: the customary invasion of the kitchen. With only a year between them, and, of similar stature and build with the same hair colour, they could easily have been taken for twins. So off they went, followed closely by Richard's younger brother Bill, and cousins Stephen and William Knight (who was always called Knight for short), leaving Richard in the drawing room with his grandparents, his father and his Uncle William.

To accommodate the two families on Christmas Day, the panelled screen, which divided the drawing room from the study, was folded back like the wings of a giant stork, to allow more room for the family gathering. This was always a light and airy room, with two windows overlooking the street at the front and two windows which looked out onto the extensive grounds at the back. The morning sunlight, reflected and intensified by the snow, streamed in through the south-facing windows of the room, showing to advantage the rich red and umber painted walls inside, hung all around with gilt-framed family portraits.

Uncle William had always loved this room when he had lived here as a boy. He stood with his back to the fire, surveying the room, ruefully looking back down the years. How he wished that *Vine House* were his!

They were all warmed, on that cold December day, by the roaring flames of a log fire. The brick fireplace, with its Italian marble surround and mantelpiece, had been built in Richard's great-grandfather's time. Constructed with Porter bricks specially made and smoothed by the craftsmen employed at the kiln, this was a solid feature at the end of the long room.

"Well, well, Richard," his grandmother was saying, "are you sickening for something?"

"No, madam. I am well, thank you."

"Do you not think Richard is sickening for something, my dear Mr Porter?" She always addressed her husband in this way.

"Hmm!" hummed his grandfather, regarding him quizzically, "I don't think so. Why do you say he is?"

"He is so quiet, so solemn."

"My dear, he is now a young man of sixteen. Not quite so acceptable to go scuttering round the house at his age."

Richard was acutely aware of a bristling in his Uncle William's demeanour. His grandfather's unwitting comparison between himself and Marshall was probably yet another thorn in Uncle William's side. Richard had seen a number of warning signs over the years. For example, he remembered that day when he had gone to Ely market with his father and Uncle William – he must only have been five or six at the time – to buy Bute and Roland, their two Suffolk punches from Mr Bailey at the horse fair. That was the day when he had first noticed his uncle's animosity and his father's unease. Richard, always considerate of others' feelings, did not wish to fuel any envy or sense of inadequacy which might still be lurking in the back of Uncle William's mind, despite his farming expertise and success.

"I have already been in Mrs Vinney's bad books today, sir. I thought that I'd better keep well out of her way!" Richard thought this white lie provided not only a viable explanation for his own unaccustomed behaviour, but also a suitable reason which would help to mollify his uncle.

"Ah yes! One must always keep on the right side of the cook. And especially a cook like Mrs Vinney!" Grandfather gesticulated widely with his arms to denote the wholesome shape of the lady in question, laughing heartily, if a little wheezily.

The love he felt for his grandfather did not obscure Richard's awareness that he was the cause of Uncle William's sense of inferiority. He rather wondered that his grandfather had failed, over the years, to see the warning signs.

By other people's standards, Uncle William was someone to be admired, someone who had been "born with a silver spoon in his mouth". It was the norm that younger sons would have to make do with a career in the ministry or as an officer in the militia or the navy, or alternatively work on the older brother's farm. Few younger sons could boast being farmers in their own right. A hundred acre tract of what used to be common land out at Hillrow had been apportioned to the Porters at the time of the Enclosure Acts. This was Uncle William's responsibility and he spared no effort to be a successful farmer, with the result that he had made a very solid financial foundation for his wife, Aunt Catherine, and their eight children.

However, all of the traditional Porter family business concerns, namely *The Maltings*, the brewery, the brick making business, two farms and *The Red Lion* coaching house, had been handed over to Henry the eldest. What is more, Henry, as the eldest, by tradition, had moved into the family home, *Vine House*.

If Richard ever had sons, they would never be given cause to feel any jealousy or rivalry. He would follow his own father's good example. For Henry treated all his children with kindness, understanding and respect for their different aptitudes, making each one believe in his own worth and his own good fortune.

One Sunday afternoon, about five years earlier, after the customary succulent roast sirloin of beef, followed by one of Mrs Vinney's delicious jam roly poly puddings, Henry had sat all the family down in the drawing room. He had stood before them.

"I have something important to say to you all. For some time your mother and I have been considering the best way of providing each of you with a good and secure future."

He addressed Richard first. Richard was then eleven years old, with three more years to go before he would finish school.

"Richard, you are a young man who values family traditions. Am I right?" he asked.

"Oh, yes indeed, Father." He had grown out of calling him "Papa".

"Your interest in the family malting business has been clear for all to see: frequent visits to the malt-house, trying to learn the trade. All this is gaining the respect of the malt-house men and boys. I would like you to take over from me as head maltster and brewer here one day."

Richard was more pleased than he could say. He stood up, proud and tall, and shook his father by the proffered hand, as a sealed bargain. This was an important moment in his life.

"Charles."

"Yes, Papa." Charles was eager and hopeful.

"You have shown yourself to have a genial character. You get on well in company and have a shrewd mind and a pleasant manner. Your mother and I consider that you are best suited to take over as the owner-landlord of our public house and coaching inn, *The Red Lion*, once you reach the age of 21. I trust this meets with your approval, that you have no objections."

"Thank you, sir." Charles had no objections whatsoever; he was content. He was naturally affable and hospitable and would be a successful publican. He also loved anything to do with horses, was already an accomplished rider, and owning a coach house would afford him opportunities to work with post horses too. Young Charles's love of animals had not gone unnoticed by Henry. Indeed, Charles was often to be found in the stable yard helping Mr Stokes.

He continued, "Also, Charles, in the mean time, I am proposing you follow a course in veterinary studies, which I am confident you will wish to develop into a lucrative sideline."

Now Charles jumped out of his seat and was shaking his father by the hand, most vigorously, for this was indeed the icing on the cake!

Bill who was eight at the time was not to be disappointed either.

"Bill, my boy, you will manage the brick-making kiln and both clay-pits. You would like that, I think, with that solid head for business on your shoulders. Running two clay pits and the kiln should be a very rewarding and secure business. With new building in the area, I can see a good future ahead."

"Thank you, Papa." He very solemnly stood before his father and they shook hands.

Ann was sitting beside her mother on the chaise longue, and baby Suzanna was being rocked gently in the crib beside them.

"Now, to the girls."

It was traditional to settle land on the husband of new brides. Although not named as such, it was in reality a dowry to attract a worthy husband. Henry Porter owned a hundred and seventy acres of land in Haddenham split between two sites: the first farm was at Haddenham End, land situated between *Vine House* and the clay pits on the outskirts of the village; and the second was at Linden End on the opposite side of the village. This was an area with a history of eel fishing in the days before the Fens were drained. In those bygone days there used to be an annual levy to the king of three thousand, three hundred and thirty-three eels as payment of taxes.

"A sizeable portion of our good farming land will be divided between Ann and Suzanna," Henry had continued. "Ann, you will receive your entitlement of land when you marry." With that, he knelt down and cupped her chin in his hand. "You will be a rich lady one day."

"Say 'thank you', child," said Alice, gently.

"Thank you, Papa," but her little voice sounded odd and dull. She did not see herself, even at that young age, as a person who would ever want a husband.

Suzanna lay oblivious to her future bounty. She slept snugly in her crocheted shawl, with her little pink thumb in her mouth.

Yes, thought Richard, on this snowy Christmas morning, in the warmth and comfort of *Vine House* drawing room, he would treat his children as fairly as his father had treated them.

Uncle William had made no similar plans for his sons, or for his daughters. William enjoyed possession of his vast arable farmlands. He would make his farm the biggest and best in the county. Already he had bought a further ten acres with outhouses and was diversifying into cattle farming. During his lifetime, he would single-handedly manage the farm. His sons would work for him; they would not be indulged. Still a staunch Cromwellian at heart who did not agree with privilege, Uncle William was a man who also espoused the French revolutionary aim of equality, now that anti-French feeling was beginning to die down. So when the time came, his sons would all inherit an equal portion of his land. However, keeping this decision to himself was to have far-reaching consequences on his family: his younger sons and daughters grew up unsure of what the future held in store for each of them, presuming that the eldest son would inherit the land and house; and Marshall, the eldest, grew up in the complacent belief that he would one day own it all.

While Marshall and Charles were tormenting Mrs Vinney during this last hour before luncheon, Richard thought of the past; and he thought about his future; and Ann Bailey who was to be Mrs Ann Porter; and he imagined his nuptial bliss; and he felt again this stirring of his emotions.

Catherine and Alice now joined the party in the drawing room, followed by the children who proudly showed off their Christmas clothes. They stood in a line for inspection. They always received such nice, kind compliments from their grandmother each year and they waited eagerly for what she would say to each of them.

Ann, however, stood with a sullen expression. She was nine years old and believed herself to be too old to stand in line with the rest. Grandmother always said the same, bland things every year: "How delightful!", "How pretty you look!", "What a lovely dress!", "The colour so brings out the natural beauty of your face!" Ann had no desire to hear what she knew to be untruths. With a peaked face and thin lips, she knew she was not attractive. She also dreaded the Christmas lunch, because she would have to sit at the side table with Jessie and Hilda and the children. Only those over the age of ten were permitted to sit at the main mahogany table with the adults.

Standing beside her was her cousin Henry, looking uncomfortable in a maroon velvet jacket and matching breeches. Beside him was cousin Jacob.

"How handsome you look, Jacob. My, my, you'll break some girl's poor heart some day!" Grandmother was already crooning.

Jacob was dreading the next Christmas. He did not mind wearing the smart sailor suit, he rather enjoyed his grandmother's comments, and Jessie always gave him an extra special hug, but next year he would be the only boy in the line of inspection. Perhaps his father would excuse him next year, so that he would not have to suffer such embarrassment.

Next in line was his sister, Edna, a strapping six-year-old who found sitting or standing still to be an impossibility. She was a pleasant-natured child, but really quite plain. Her pink frock only accentuated her puppy fat and her chubby cheeks.

Grandmother was undeterred, "My, my, what a lovely dress! Don't your cheeks look even rosier than ever! Quite delightful!"

Then there was Suzanna, her excitement now beginning to reach a crescendo. She looked very pretty in her pale blue frilly dress with its creamy-white organza sash and bow. Her fair hair had been curled in tapers for this special occasion, and now her face was delicately framed with golden ringlets.

Richard thought of chestnut curls framing a lovely face, as his grandmother continued her string of compliments.

At the end of the line were his youngest cousins. Mary, aged four, held her little sister's hand. Rachel was only two and looked as if she might cry. Grandmother looked wistful and a little tearful too.

"Pretty as a picture!" There was a slight tremor in her voice. Richard knew she was thinking about her own two little girls who had died in infancy.

"My dear cousins," he coaxed, "go and give your grandmother a kiss!" He did not want his grandmother to be sad today. As she embraced the two children, she looked over towards Richard and smiled gratefully. He was a good boy. He would make some young girl very happy indeed!

There was a loud, prolonged rap on the drawing room door. It had been eagerly awaited. The five remaining boys made a grand entrance. Bill joined hands with his cousin Marshall to form an arch, while cousin Knight and cousin Stephen formed a second arch. Through this came Charles into the centre of the room, saying,

"Ladies and gentlemen, Mrs Vinney has an announcement."

It was tradition that Cook would enter the drawing room on special occasions to announce that lunch was ready to be served. She had taken off her aprons, and had donned a special Belgian lace mop cap. Louisa and Clara were in the dining room standing straight, having taken up position to assist Mrs Vinney to wait at table. They looked smart in newly starched white aprons and caps. Mrs Vinney walked almost imperiously through the archway, her hands folded neatly somewhere under her bosom, resting on her spreading stomach.

"Mrs Porter, madam," she addressed the lady of the house, as was the custom. "Lunch is served."

There were sounds of small feet scampering up and down stairs, doors opening and shutting in quick succession, and whoops and shrieks of the children playing "Hunt the Slipper". This Christmas game had been played every year in *Vine House* for as long as anyone could remember. Grandfather was now seated in the drawing room beside the fire, cupping his hands round his brandy glass, inhaling the rising fumes of his warming post-prandial drink.

"Every year it takes me back, you know. I remember, when I was a boy, we used to play 'Hunt the Slipper'. Without fail!"

Grandfather had been saying those very words for as long as anyone could remember too!

Richard, Charles and Marshall were too old for this boisterous game. Indeed, as all three had now left school and were "working men", they had remained behind in the dining room with their grandfather and their respective fathers to enjoy a glass of vintage port, before joining the ladies in the drawing room.

Grandfather had chuckled, "Have the ladies retired to the drawing room, or have they withdrawn to the retiring room?" He never seemed to tire of his simple play on words, and his listeners never gave the impression that they had heard it before, many times!

On Christmas afternoon as the sky was darkening, the drawing room window drapes were always drawn to in readiness for the Porter family Christmas concert. This annual event was always performed at the far end of the room on a raised stage erected each Christmas Eve. Green velvet drapes were hung on the far wall, as a backdrop, and the lighting had been set up.

Alice had directed operations. "Now, Louisa, place the two oil lamps one at either side 'downstage'."

"How do you mean, ma'am?" Louisa looked nonplussed. Having never been to a theatre, she did not understand the thespian terminology.

"At the front of the stage." On the one hand, Alice might have appeared formidable to her staff, but on the other, she was patient and did her best to instruct them, though just how Louisa would benefit from the knowledge of theatrical terms was debatable!

The oil lamps were placed strategically on a whatnot each, and a further two lamps were set up on two low occasional tables just near enough to the front of the platform to augment the illumination of the family members who were to perform a party piece.

Rehearsals during December had brought tears and frustration, but through practice and help from Jessie and Hilda in their respective households, the performers were ready. On numerous visits to Grandmother's attic, where the air was musty from the tired perfume of old lavender sachets, the grandchildren had carefully selected costumes and accessories from her oak chest where she stored all manner of fancy dress garments and accessories.

"Take good care," she always said, in order to prevent any rough rummaging through the chest. "This is my family heirloom," she would proudly announce each year. "Some of these clothes are two hundred years old."

Indeed, some of the silk fabrics were very fragile and frayed, and some of the woollen garments had suffered from an attack of dust moths, but each of the young performers always eventually came away with something to suit the occasion.

The sounds of "Hunt the Slipper" had gradually died down and it was supposed that the children were now upstairs donning their costumes. Richard, Marshall and Charles excused themselves from the company in the drawing room, for they too were to dress up in preparation for the show. While Hilda took the toddler Rachel, now fretful, to the nursery for her customary afternoon nap, Jessie helped the young children to dress up. They would have liked nothing better than to have seen their young charges perform, but this was exclusively a family time and the two of them would join Mrs Vinney, Louisa and Clara in the warm kitchen for a glass of wine, mince pies and hot roasted chestnuts.

What a motley yet colourful group entered the drawing room! Twelve of them filed in, like a troupe of strolling players from mediaeval times. They took their seats around the room. Grandmother was as excited as a small child.

"Oh Mr Porter, my dear," she piped, putting the palms of her hands together below her chin. "What a pretty sight! Just like wandering minstrels." Now she was clapping her fingers together in agitated anticipation of the pleasure in store. The programme of entertainment was about to begin.

The hosts of *Vine House*, by tradition, began the proceedings. Alice, who was to accompany Henry, sat down at their newly acquired pianoforte in its exquisite walnut casing. The ancient virginal, which it had replaced, now stood in the nursery in the corner, but not abandoned, for this was where Ann, already a technically proficient musician, would regularly practise her scales. Henry held his head high, placed his right hand on what Alice would term his "corporation" and, taking a deep breath, prepared to sing. He had a fine, bass voice which resonated through the room, as he sang the four verses of a Robert Burns's poem, which had recently been put to music,

"My love is like a red, red rose
That's newly sprung in June
My love is like a melody
That's sweetly played in tune.
As fair art thou my bonnie lass
So deep in love am I:

And I will love thee still, my dear,
Till a' the seas gang dry."

It was plain for all to see, during the rendition of these first two verses, that this was more than just a song for Henry to sing at a party. This was a personalised love song to his wife. While he sang the last two verses, Grandmother's eyes glistened and Grandfather nodded his approval. Richard, his own heart ablaze with his newly found love for Ann Bailey, was suddenly aware of the ardent love which his parents felt for one another. Like most young people, he was quite shocked at this revelation. He found himself imagining his father and mother alone in their bedroom at night, love-making. He was endeavouring to reconcile this new, hitherto unsuspected, perception of his parents with the old, more staid and stereotypical image.

Amidst the applause, Knight and his younger brothers and sisters were preparing for their performance. Knight stood at the side of the apron stage, with a scroll, which he was opening in preparation to read. He was to be the narrator of the schoolboys' favourite ballad, *Sir Patrick Spens*. Cousin Henry was dressed flamboyantly in a large golden cape as the King of Dunfermline town, with a goblet in his left hand. Later, he was to divest himself of his cape with a carefully rehearsed, swirling motion, and become the "skeely skipper", Sir Patrick Spens himself. Eight-year-old Jacob was weighed down with a helmet, sword and shield. He had been noisily manoeuvring himself into position on a stool beside Henry, for he was to play the role of the loyal but ancient knight who "sat at the king's right knee". Edna and Mary, golden combs in their hair, were seated together as the ladies who were to lose their loved ones at the end of the sad tale. Each child presently was engaged in demurely fanning herself with one of Grandmother's "heirloom" fans.

"The King sits in Dunfermline toon," began Knight, aware of the power he had as story-teller. At ten years old he was a strong lad, who had decided long ago that he was destined to

follow in his father's footsteps and be a successful and respected farmer. Had he understood his father's psyche, he would have made earlier plans to achieve his goal. As it was, he almost left it too late.

"*Drinking the blude-red wine.*"

Young Henry raised the goblet to his lips and supped imaginary wine with an uncommonly noisy, slurping sound. Lowering the said vessel, he shouted with what he considered to be the voice of Scottish royalty,

"'*O where will I get a skeely skipper*
To sail this gude ship o' mine?'"

Knight, flinching slightly, continued his narration and on the words *Up and spake an eldern knight, sat at the king's right knee*, Jacob fairly propelled himself from his stool, to say his words *Sir Patrick Spens is the best sailor that ever sailed the sea.* Once standing, he metamorphosed into an old man. He completely overacted his role as the elderly knight, his voice trembling with age, his armour rattling, and his sword shaking in his hand at the end of a crooked, outstretched arm.

There was a fierce, if chaotic, enactment of the storm at sea as Sir Patrick Spens and his men were drowned. Henry and Jacob had looked forward to this energetic part of their performance. There was much staggering, much spluttering and choking from Henry, while Jacob clattered and clanged in his armour, as he gyrated in an agonised fall. They died a terrible death, writhing uncontrollably and twitching sporadically on the ground, before they were finally still!

Edna and Mary, with a nod from Knight, began a boo-hooing, a little too gusty for his liking, but the final lines were upon him, and he wished to end with an impressive flourish.

"*Half-ower, half-ower, to Aberdour*
'*Tis fifty fathom deep;*
And there lies gude Sir Patrick Spens,
Wi' the Scots lords at his feet."

Alice was busy in the corner of the room stuffing a cushion up inside the back of Richard's Elizabethan doublet. Still an avid reader with a penchant for stories of adventure and heroic deeds, Richard had told his brothers and cousins that he was to perform one of Shakespeare's famous speeches. He was ready to go on stage. The younger members of his audience were waiting expectantly for a regal, dramatic figure to come striding onto the boards. They were not expecting what they saw: a humped back, a seemingly shrivelled arm and a head lolling to one side. He was, of course, in role as the evil "crooked figure" of Richard III, doing justice to Shakespeare's portrayal of an out and out villain.

"Now is the winter of our discontent
Made glorious summer by this sun of York..."

Miss Ruby Arber, Richard's teacher at the Arkenstall School for Boys, would have approved. She liked a good, rousing delivery of Shakespearian speeches. Alice and Henry were demonstrably proud of their eldest son, and listened intently as King Richard tried to play upon the audience's sympathy:

"I, that am curtail'd of this fair proportion,
Cheated of feature by dissembling Nature,
Deform'd, unfinish'd, sent before my time
Into this breathing world, scarce half made up,
And that so lamely and unfashionable,
That dogs bark at me as I halt by them..."

However, when Richard growled, *"I am determined to prove a villain,"* going on to outline his murderous intentions, the assembled Porter family were suitably stunned and horrified.

When Richard took a bow at the end of this speech, they were unsure whether to applaud or not, but when he stood up straight, the contorted evil countenance of King Richard now replaced by his own familiar warm smile, they clapped and cheered with all their might.

Richard stepped down to make way for his cousin Stephen who looked almost unrecognisable in his grandfather's discarded grey wig.

"Periwig-pated, periwig-pated!" Grandfather chirped to his wife, enjoying this alliterative saying, which had been a favourite of his grandfather's.

"Do be quiet, Mr Porter, my dear, for that's the wig you used to wear," admonished Grandmother, but very quietly so that only those with keen hearing nearby could have heard.

The said wig was far too big for Stephen. It perched akimbo and balanced precariously on his left ear. Poor Stephen, who was not at all partial to public performance, wished that the stage would open and swallow him up right there and then. His young sisters began to titter, but were nudged to silence by Knight.

Stephen launched into a speech which William Penn had made to the Pilgrim Fathers, as they set foot on their new land. The performance was saved from mediocrity by Stephen's love of all things American, and Grandmother was discerning enough to suspect that this grandson of hers would "go a-roving" one day.

The assembled group thought Grandfather was about to breathe his last, during the Sailors' *Hornpipe* danced by Bill. Aided and abetted by his mother at the pianoforte, and dressed as Jack Tar, his rope-pulling actions and his heel-toe steps began as the regular, popular dance routine. By arrangement, his mother steadily increased the tempo. The faster the music, the more frantic became Bill's *Hornpipe*. Grandmother felt quite dizzy watching the ever-increasing speed of his arms, and his feet positively became a blur. The children were doubled up with fits of uncontrollable hysterics, and Grandfather laughed so heartily that he was quite overcome with a fit of coughing.

Once the children had settled and Grandfather had wiped his eyes, Marshall and Charles, looking identical with their blond hair, and dressed in similar costumes as love-sick poets, moved with military precision towards the chaise longue where their respective mothers were sitting. At exactly the same time and with exactly the same actions, Marshall knelt before Catherine and solemnly took her hand and Charles knelt before Alice and solemnly took her hand. At first it had seemed as if this was to be yet another humorous turn, and Henry and Jacob prepared themselves for more noisy hilarity, but a hush descended on everyone in the room as Marshall and Charles began to recite the gentle verses, which Michael Drayton had written on the night before he died.

"So well I love thee as without thee I
Love nothing..."

With his new-found feelings, Richard was immediately struck with the absolute truth of these words. It was as if they had been written only for him.

"...if I might choose, I'd rather die
Than be one day debarred thy company."

Alice was smiling, enjoying her role in this creditable performance by her son, and Henry in his turn smiled to show his approbation. Yes, he had been right: Charles was indeed a genial fellow.

"Since beast and plant do grow and live and move,
Beasts are those men that such a life approve:
He only lived that deadly is in love."

Aunt Catherine was smiling also, but she looked a little too deeply into the eyes of her eldest son, kneeling before her. Her love for her finely-featured, good-looking son, a living Adonis, was all too transparent. One may wonder at her naivety, but not condemn. Had she been more worldly-wise, she would have behaved a little more circumspectly, but she was an uncomplicated woman who knew nothing of the art of dissembling. She simply adored her children. Equally, she adored her husband. Catherine was above all a good wife who had borne her husband eight children.

"So all my thoughts are pieces but of you,

Which put together makes a glass so true
As I therein no other's face but yours can view."

At these closing words, had Richard not been so engrossed with thoughts of love for Ann Bailey, he would have noticed Uncle William's stony expression. Marshall, the eldest son, the apple of his mother's eye, had gone too far.

The last item on the programme came all too soon with little Suzanna singing *The Holly and the Ivy* accompanied on the pianoforte by her sister Ann. To her piano tutor, this accompaniment would be deemed accurate, but to a sensitive ear, it was a trifle too mechanical. To be fair, Ann was more comfortable in the nursery, practising her chromatic scales and arpeggios on the virginal, and, although she had acquiesced readily to her mother's request that she accompany her young sister, she would rather not have come under the gaze and scrutiny of the extended family. However, Suzanna's sweet, soprano voice easily made up in warmth what the accompaniment lacked.

She clasped her small hands together and began to sing,
"The holly and the ivy
When they are both full grown..."

Ann joined in the singing of the refrain after each verse. Her voice was beginning to move towards an alto pitch, possessing a musicality hitherto unsuspected by the family group. The voices of the two girls blended together, and when Ann sang the descant to the refrain, then the carol acted as a spur for others to sing. At the end of the fifth verse, even Grandmother's warbling treble could be heard under the impromptu choral melange. By the last verse, everyone was in full voice as they reached a resounding crescendo:
"With the rising of the sun
And the coming of the deer,
And the playing of the merry organ
Sweet singing in the choir."

When Richard slipped into bed that night, he could still hear the last chorus of *The Holly and the Ivy* being sung ever so softly. Whether or not these were real voices, or simply musical strains in the imagination, was not too clear, for Richard was in a comfortable, warm and soporific daze. The occasional "sshh!" from Ann and a giggle or two from Suzanna, Edna and Mary convinced him, at last, that he was still awake.

It was the custom for Uncle William and Aunt Catherine to stay at *The Red Lion* on Christmas night, along with their older boys. Cousin Edna and Cousin Mary stayed over in Ann and Suzanna's room, much to Ann's annoyance. As things stood, her young sister was an encumbrance which she had no alternative but to tolerate, but her patience was stretched to the limit when she was forced to share their bed with her two young cousins, especially Edna who could not stand still, nor sit still, nor lie still.

"Why do they have to stay?" she had asked her mother rather fitfully on Christmas Eve.

"Because it is Christmas. Remember the story of the innkeeper who took in Joseph and Mary. That was charity, Ann. You would do well to remember the shining Christian message."

So Ann had been silenced and a little chastened too. Nevertheless, Christmas night, it seemed to Ann, was more of an unjust punishment, and she found that the Christian message was altogether rather dim!

Richard could hear no sound whatsoever from the nursery across the landing from his bedroom. It had been deemed expedient for Hilda to stay at *Vine House*. She presently slept soundly on the sofa in the nursery with her charge, two-year old Cousin Rachel, in the cot beside her. Rachel was a placid little thing, who liked the peace and quiet of her times with her nurse, Hilda. Large gatherings and attention always made her fretful, as was apparent when she stood before her Grandmother during the inspection before luncheon. Being the focus of attention would continue to be an anathema to Rachel for the rest of her life.

Before Richard and his father had escorted Grandmother and Grandfather back to their house, Grandmother had helped to prepare Boxing Day gifts which Alice would distribute the following day. Grandmother admired this daughter-in-law who found time to raise a family, see to the smooth running of the household, helped to supervise the sixteen men and fourteen boys who were employed in *The Maltings* and the Brewery. Alice always took the time to fulfil her benevolent role, expected of women of means in the parish, to present St Stephen's Day gifts to the families of these employees.

"Are you sure that you should step foot outside tomorrow, my dear Alice?" Grandmother had asked, for the snow lay thick on the ground with no sign of a thaw.

Alice was not a woman to be daunted. Hers was a strong and fighting spirit. "Of course I shall go," she had said. "I go every year without fail. It will be a sad day when weather usurps tradition, do you not think?"

Richard now recalled, with a degree of pride, the accuracy of his aim, as Stephen yelped and scooped snow from inside his collar. Uncle William had been busy helping Aunt Catherine through the crunching snow to *The Red Lion*. Three rooms had been warmed in readiness for them and for their five sons, as was the custom on Christmas night. Needless to say, there had been a snowball fight of epic proportions between the cousins. Richard and his two brothers faced Marshall, Stephen and their three brothers, in what seemed at first to be a stand-off. The young men had eyed each other across the street; they had bent down to form snowballs; they had stood up and taken aim with a precision which the Duke of Wellington himself would have acclaimed. Then they had fired mercilessly on the enemy!

But in contrast to the memories of these boyish games, the thoughts of Ann Bailey came flooding into Richard's mind, as he lay under the coverlets, the flames from the fire projecting a kaleidoscope of flickering images on the walls. He had tried all day to focus on the Christmas proceedings, but time and again, in his mind's eye, he saw her standing there in Holy Trinity church, smiling to him. When he closed his eyes now, he completely succumbed to her allure. He pictured her pretty face, framed with chestnut curls.

He thought of the future and what it would hold.

So well I love thee as without thee I love nothing were the words he whispered as he finally fell asleep.

Chapter 4

MARSHALL

15th April 1840

Dawn on another windless day. The early morning April showers left the land shimmering with opalescence, as shafts of the sunlight revealed the unchanging beauty of the fenland vistas. One might have even begun to suspect that time had stood still in these familiar environs of Haddenham, until a distant throbbing sound was heard.

Looking towards the Great Mill, now with a slim chimney built alongside it, one could not but notice that the sails were turning. No longer at the mercy of the wind, this mechanism for scooping water to the higher delph, like so many others in the fenland, boasted a steam-powered beam-engine. Forward-thinking farmers had no doubt that this innovation was economically essential for their survival in those times of agricultural depression. They could not afford for their land to be inundated, year after year, with crops ruined and the ground unworkable for at least the following season.

In counterbalance to these arguments of a solid, financial foundation, there were many old-timers who deplored the new steam-powered beam-engines.

On the previous Saturday evening, we would have overheard a conversation on this very topic. Bob Sears had been complaining to his life-long friend Thomas Thripley, as they were sitting beside the fire in the snuggery of *The Plough*. He looked grave as he sucked on his clay pipe.

"Why they had to demolish Neville's Mill, I'll never know," he leant forward.

"There wasn't enough wind for the two on 'em!" Thomas offered this stale observation, nodding wisely notwithstanding.

"But look what they've put in its place! It's unnatural." Bob was getting worked up. This was a favourite hobby-horse of his. "All them pulsating pistons. It was never as nature intended."

It had seemed to Thomas that it was in his best interests to agree with his friend who was tending towards apoplexy. "Ay, and that roar of steam. At Great Mill, so they say, a body cannot hear himself think with all the noise."

The landlord, Fred Metcalfe had come over with a refill of ale in a pewter pitcher always used for the purpose of replenishing the tankards of those seated in the snuggery.

"So you don't hold much store by the invention of steam power, then?" he had asked, more as a matter of being friendly in the manner of all hospitable landlords. He had not been prepared for Bob's excessively irate reply.

"You know what, Fred? I wish that Thomas Newcomen had never been born. I wish that James Watt had never been born. All this messin' about with their new 'steamers'. If they was both here, I would string 'em up! That I would! On the gallows!" With that he had sat back on his chair, red-faced, and taken another draw on his pipe.

Thomas had thought the best policy was to take to considering the old days, "Yes, the old wind-engines was best. There was something wholesome about the creak of the sails turnin' in the wind."

Looking in the direction of William's farm down at Hillrow, it could be seen that his old wooden wind-engine with its thirty scoops had been replaced by a modern construction. An eighty horse-power beam-engine had been erected two years before, and William's ambition to have the biggest and the best farm was fast becoming a reality, as his land had been almost totally drained and productivity increased dramatically. While some farmers in the Fens preferred windmills which employed scoop-wheels, because they were more familiar to the operators when it came to maintenance, William had opted for the more modern pump which the more progressive engineers had advised.

However, the condemnation in *The Plough* of the noise issuing from the "steamers" was not just an old man's gripe about all things modern. The constant throbbing noise emanating from the pump house situated not twenty yards from William's farm at Hillrow was indeed so great that even Catherine, the epitome of complacent contentment, had complained of headaches and a "distraction which she found hard to bear". William, ever wishing to please his paragon of a wife, had been quick to act. Within three months, a new Victorian house, with extensive stabling and outhouses, had been erected on Main Street in Haddenham, and that is where we will now find him and his family happily in residence.

Unfortunately, not all movements of the populace were as successful. The newspapers told of the general exodus from the rural areas to the towns, because it had become more and more difficult for the small farmer to eke out a living. They could not compete with the large farms such as those of the Reads, the Cockles, the Grangers and the Porters, whose use of every modern advancement in mechanised farming had led to improved management of agricultural land.

Bob Sears and Thomas Thripley were two such small farmers in their day.

"I remember the days when we could make a living out of two cows, one horse and a pig," said Thomas. It was his turn now to take the initiative. He shook his head sadly, and then supped long and deep from his ale.

"My mother always kept a pig specially for the pot," Bob remembered. "The trouble we had killing 'em too. Why, I remember the first time my brother and I had to do it. We weren't no more than nine or ten. We ran round and round the yard thirty times or more after Moll, I think we called her, till we was all out of breath, with a stitch in our sides. Moll was puffin' and pantin' so much we thought we wouldn't need to stick her at all. My brother, Samuel, you remember 'im, lay his full weight on her, and I roped her feet." Bob exhaled loudly as he recalled the sheer exertion of the experience. "What a weight she were to drag into the barn, and even harder to haul up over the beam, I can tell you. 'Slit her throat! Slit her throat!' Samuel kept shouting, for Moll's squeals was that terrible to hear. So I did." He shuddered as he remembered Moll's head hanging down, blood spurting into the pail beneath.

"Ay, Samuel," sighed Thomas nostalgically. "He were such a bright lad. He's long gone now, eh, Bob. He must be dead sixty years, if it's a day."

"Sixty-one years, three months and four days." Bob knew to the very day, for Samuel had been his twin brother, who had died on their thirteenth birthday, during the 1779 outbreak of cholera.

Small farmers, in their thousands, had been forced to leave their tied cottages and seek employment in the towns where the factories offered the promise of security for themselves and for their families. Haddenham lost scores of such farmers during the twenties and thirties, many of them travelling to the north-west of England where the cotton mills beckoned, and many to the north-east where the coal-mines invitingly smiled.

For those who went in search of this bright new future, there had been no change in living standards. Every so often, word got back to relatives, of terrible working conditions, back-to-back squalid housing, inadequate sanitation, the stink of sewage running in the streets, disease and poverty: sad stories of wholesale disappointment and near betrayal. Those left behind were helpless. All they could do was shake their heads and offer such platitudinous proverbs as "Out of the frying pan into the fire".

But there were some things in Haddenham which never changed.

64

Each January, the unemployed young farm labourers of the village would go from house to house in the hope of collecting alms to help them through the cold wintry weeks ahead; this was almost a last ditch attempt to survive, before they too were pushed into the decision to uproot and leave in search of a better life.

Each May the young girls, who were caught in a poverty-trap, less able than their brothers to go to distant counties to find employment, would stop rich ladies at the Mayday fair asking for a farthing, to buy ribbons for their hair to "go a-courting", with the ultimate aim of catching a husband. During the past two years, there had been a move by the "Peelers", the newly arrived police force in the area, to eradicate begging in the street, but on this particular day, they turned a blind eye to a young girl's outstretched palm, excusing it as a kind of ritualised begging, belonging to the unwritten catalogue of unchanging village traditions.

On Saint Thomas's Day, better known here as Goodening Day, the parish widows still visited the rich households, never failing to call at the Porter houses: Alice Porter continued to give each woman a packet of tea, rumoured now to be medicinally beneficial, as well as being something refined to drink out of china cups on special occasions; Catherine Porter always bought in a range of preserved figs and oriental spices to donate, which she did with a natural, gentle grace.

Already the goodening ladies were looking forward to calling on Ann Bailey, who was to be the new Mrs Porter, in the white-washed house at the end of the town towards Linden End. By all accounts, following in the Porter family tradition, she should be as generous and kind as her mother-in-law.

Outside William's new residence on Main Street, the carriage was waiting to take all the family to Wilberton Church to the first Porter wedding of the new generation. Young Mr Porter of Haddenham parish was to be joined in holy matrimony with Mistress Ann Bailey of the parish of Wilberton.

Marshall, for the first time in his life, was apprehensive of the role that he must play during this important day of family celebration.

"Ooh, sir, you look a treat!" Janet, the house-servant, stood almost open-mouthed in admiration of her employer's eldest son. Marshall at twenty-four could have swept any young maiden off her feet.

Janet always said what she thought, a quality which had led her into much mischief in the past, but it had also led to her good fortune. Had she not worn her heart on her sleeve when "walking out" with her young man John Stokes, the second of the Stokes brothers, then she would never have secured him for a husband, for he was diffident and unassuming.

Marshall had the air and grace of a very fine gentleman in the attire he chose to wear, whatever the function, whatever the pastime. Today was no exception. He looked at his reflection in the long Queen Anne mirror, which stood on the spacious landing. Refracted rays of sunlight streamed in through the stained glass window at the far end. As the rainbow hues danced on him, Marshall was pleased with what he saw: he looked the very essence of the "man about town" in the clothes he was to wear at the wedding. From the crisp white stock wound deftly round his neck, kept in place with a twenty-four carat gold neck-pin, down to his highly-polished black patent leather dress shoes, he looked exactly what he was: a rich man's son.

He worked hard at keeping up appearances. The outer impression of suavity and easy confidence would mask his inner-most sense of his own inadequacy. He felt all too keenly his lack of worth, in his father's eyes. Since leaving school ten years earlier, his father had given him no responsibility for any aspect of the running of the Hillrow estate. Marshall had tried, in those early days of so-called employment, to learn as much about farming as was possible, only to be blocked by a father who regarded his son's efforts as usurping his own position of power. By now he recognised his father's selfish pride in having total control, as well as his inability to delegate or to share. He foresaw that these would ever be insurmountable obstacles to his gleaning the essentials about good farm management, and had consequently abandoned his efforts.

Stephen, a couple of years younger than Marshall, had been irked by similar frustrations. Just last week he had confided in his brother.

"God knows, I have tried, Marshall," he had complained, "but it is no earthly use. The first opportunity I get, I will be on *The Great Western* ship. America is the place for me. To make my fortune."

The Great Western was one of Brunel's new advanced steam ships with paddles. Her maiden voyage across the Atlantic had been in 1838 when she sailed from Bristol, arriving in New York on the very same day as *The Sirius*, a seven hundred ton steam paddle ship, which had sailed from the Irish port of Cork.

"It is a big step to take," said Marshall. "Too much to risk. Too much at stake." His tone was far from one of encouragement. The fact is that, despite all, he enjoyed the kudos of being the son of one of the most respected and successful farmers in the county. If his father could not trust him enough to give him responsibility, so be it: he was at least secure in the knowledge that one day he would inherit the one hundred and thirty acre Hillrow estate.

Stephen, however, was not one to be discouraged. He was made of sterner stuff. "What else is there to do? I have no expectations here. The farm and all the land will be yours, and the rest of us, instead of being dependent on Father will be dependent on you. What sort of future is that?"

Marshall was only too aware of the fact that Stephen, like him, lacked skill and training, so all he could envisage for his brother was a life of insecurity and poverty on alien and inhospitable shores.

"What will you do?" he asked pointedly, but he was worried too.

"Fruit-farming!"

"Fruit-farming!" Marshall scoffed.

"You have always disparaged my American books, but I have been reading about Florida. That is the place to go: huge areas of land going for a few pence an acre, with government subsidies to help settlers set up in farming. So, I shall save all my allowance, and I will be on that ship."

"That will take years."

"As long as it takes! As long as it takes!" Stephen emphatically held his chin up, with his jaws set. He would not be deterred from his life's plan.

Marshall secretly was in awe of this kind of dedication. He knew in his heart of hearts that such a trait could never be part of his own make-up. He enjoyed living for the moment, and spending his allowance was one of his greatest pleasures. He had taken full advantage of his freedom from responsibility, and enjoyed a life of luxury, doing whatever he wished. He knew that his extravagance was already the talk of the village, but he also knew that by presenting himself as a man of means he could not fail to win admirers. As he looked at himself in the glass, he prided himself on his dashing appearance. He sighed with pleasure, as he considered how many a likely lass had had her eye on him over the past few years as a possible husband, and how many a shopkeeper in the town had worked hard to secure their daughters' future happiness, by showering him with credit and favour on the principle that they "would reap what they would sow".

However, by the time he had descended to the hallway and was about to enter the front room, his confidence began to wane. His mother would be there, but so too would his father, the man with whom he shared nothing. Theirs was a stale relationship, bordering on mutual dislike. Marshall took a deep breath, put on his accustomed act of ease and assurance, and entered the room.

Resplendent in a plum-coloured velvet gown, at forty-seven, Catherine could easily have been taken for a woman ten years younger. With her fair hair, blue eyes, and natural elegance, she looked more like Marshall's sister. He genuinely admired his mother's looks and, with an unforced charm, he said so.

"My dear Mother," he smiled as he took her right hand in his and kissed her long fingers, "I pity the bride today, for many heads will turn instead to look at you. Father, is she not a picture of perfection."

William's square-set face was becoming florid, but he attempted a smile.

"Yes indeed," were the only words that he could manage to utter. He was torn between his ardent love for his wife, whose affections he jealously guarded, and a surging anger at yet another display of his son's seductive gallantry.

Just as Catherine reached up to stroke her eldest son's blond hair, Stephen and Knight saved the day by entering the room, in their new suits which had been tailor made in Cambridge, along with Marshall's, for this special occasion. Catherine was beside herself with the pride and joy of motherhood, as she beheld these attractive and virile young men who were her sons.

Following closely on their heels were the three girls, who wore identical blue satin dresses and straw bonnets tied with blue ribbon. Edna at fourteen had still not lost her puppy fat: indeed she was a thick-set girl, physically more like her father. She looked ill-at-ease in her blue satin dress, the bodice of which tightly flattened her developing breasts to an embarrassing and somewhat painful degree, but she was a pleasant and lively girl, who had determined that as soon as possible she would make her grandmother's prognostications come true: she would "make some young man a very good wife". She was looking forward to today's family wedding to find out what actually happened during a marriage ceremony!

John Stokes had brought the family's shining, black carriage from the coach house, through the ornate coaching arch, round to the front of the house. William had always had a high opinion of the Stokes family, and he had taken John into his employ some five years earlier, at the same time as he had employed his wife, Sarah, as a house-servant. They were a solid, reliable couple. When John had suggested that his younger brother Simon should drive the second coach to Wilberton church, William had acceded to the proposition with no misgivings.

Once the younger boys had raced each other down stairs and burst into the front room, in all their finery let it be said, amidst parental admonitions of "Be careful!" and "Behave like gentlemen, if you please!", the family were ready to set off in the direction of Wilberton Parish Church.

Marshall's façade of confidence was beginning to drop at the thought of the day ahead. He dreaded what the next hour alone would bring. His cousin Richard would be there. Richard, who had once been his friend, had been the bane of his life over the past months. And he knew, with a certainty borne of an experience of life well beyond his years, that Richard would be there outside the church, lying in wait, ready to challenge. Yes, wedding or no wedding, it was a day to be fraught with family divisions.

He sat back in the carriage, trying to regain his composure. He must strive to remain calm with his usual panache. In ten minutes he would be there.

When Marshall and his family arrived at the church door, Richard was already there. Marshall's apprehensions about a possible confrontation with Richard began to evaporate when he found that his cousin was busily engaged in helping Grandmother into her bath chair. She had grown "rheumaticky" she said, and the comfort of this invalid vehicle was a great solace to her, and it also ensured the

70

attention which she craved. Since Grandfather's death two years earlier, she had lost her sparkle and her interest in present day happenings.

Today's wedding, for example, was altogether confusing: she wasn't quite sure which of her grandsons was getting married. Was it Marshall? Or was it Richard? Either way, they both seemed to her to be far too young for marriage. They were no more than children! Had she been clear in her thoughts, she would have recalled that she had been no more than a slip of a girl when she had married, and her Henry had been no more than twenty-two. Now, after fifty-five years of a comfortable and satisfactory marriage, she missed her husband's predicable comic sayings and his homely ways. She was lonely and old, in a world which was leaving her behind.

Marshall got on with the business of welcoming the Porter and Bailey families and seeing that they were warmly welcomed and ushered to their designated seats, the Baileys on the left of the aisle and the Porters on the right, as was the custom. Richard had disappeared into the gloom of the church to settle Grandmother in one of the right-hand pews beside Uncle Henry and Aunt Alice. So far, the anticipated friction between him and his cousin had been averted.

It had not always been like this between them. Well he remembered their boyhood days when they were as thick as thieves. How he had looked forward to his weekly visit to the *Vine House* nursery when they were no more than six or seven, when Jessie would tell them stories of adventure, roundly scold them when their tumbling play-fights became rough, and wag her finger when Marshall became too flamboyant and noisy.

"Master Marshall," she would say, "If you don't behave in a more decorous fashion, I shall have to marshall you home!" She had always loved her little joke! He grew to love it too.

Richard and he had enjoyed such times together: so many escapades. He grew quite nostalgic as he remembered one Easter Sunday when they, aged about eleven, had gone fishing for eels over at Grunty Fen. The little rowing boat from which they fished had overturned and they had scrambled to safety, clinging to tufts of marsh grass as they hauled themselves out of the brown water. It was an adventure and a half! They had been nearly sick with fright, but how they had laughed afterwards, as they stripped off their clothes to wring them out, yet both fearing what their parents would say when they heard that a boat had sunk and that they had nearly drowned.

And then there was the time when they were eighteen and they had gone to the evening fair on Hospital Sunday. This was one of the Haddenham highlights of the year, when people would congregate in their hundreds. The band was playing, and there were all manner of trifles to be won at coconut shies and at hoopla stalls. The fortune-teller's tent was like a magnet, and Marshall and Richard had queued for a quarter of an hour before finally paying their threepence to have their future foretold. Inside the gloom, a wizened old crone had sat hunched over a table with a fringed red cloth spread over it. Richard had dug Marshall in the ribs to stop him from laughing out loud. What with the hooped earrings, the brass candlesticks and the crystal ball, it was really too stereotypical for anyone to take seriously, but they had sat down at the table together, and listened to what she had to say.

She had looked at Marshall and croaked, "I see a long and happy life."

Marshall had been ready to burst. This was just too predictable.

"Go on!" he managed to say in a serious tone, despite wanting to laugh outright.

She had peered into her crystal ball as if it were the fount of all destiny, but said nothing.

"Go on!" Marshall urged her, for he, like us all, harboured a nagging suspicion that there just might be truth in what fortune-tellers had to say. Nostradamus, after all, had been proved to be right about the pestilence of 1832, when hundreds had died in Ely and Doctor Muriel had nearly been driven to an early grave looking after so many patients suffering from cholera.

Then the old crone had broken into a semi-chant, "You will gain what your heart desires, but your heart will desire to gain."

"What does that mean?" he had demanded to know. He disliked riddles and guessing games. However, he was not destined to be satisfied, for she had turned to Richard.

With no hesitation she reached out and took his hand in hers. Looking at his upturned palm, she said, "I see a full circle."

Marshall had wanted to laugh, but Richard had looked thoughtfully at her, as if he believed every word.

"But beware! I see family divisions."

She then had cupped her hands round her crystal ball and once again chanted, "You will lose what your heart desires, but your heart will desire what you choose."

As they emerged from the tent, Richard had snapped out of his near reverie. "Look! There are the Bailey girls."

Always eager to meet young maidens, Marshall had said, "Well, what dashed pretty girls! Where did they spring from?"

"Wilberton. They are the Baileys of Wilberton! You know, Richard Bailey, the stud farmer." Richard had shaken his head and patted Marshall playfully on the shoulder. "If you attended church more regularly, you would have seen them long before now. I meet them every Sunday."

It was true that, like his parents, Marshall rarely attended church. Christmas and funerals, that was all! He had been christened Church of England in Holy Trinity church, but, as his parents had decided against child baptism for Marshall's younger brothers and sisters, religious belief was not high on the agenda in William and Catherine's household. His parents had not even had a church wedding, he seemed to recall.

"We talk after morning service," Richard had continued. "Very pleasant company they are too."

Marshall had taken the initiative. "Come on! I think introductions are in order. A foursome would be most agreeable."

He had been all ready to march forward and introduce himself, and was a little taken aback when Richard had taken the lead.

"Miss Bailey, Miss Margaret, good evening. I trust you are both well?" Richard was always one to keep to the correct formalities of address, by referring to the older of the two by her title of "Miss Bailey", and only when she married would her younger sister, Margaret, adopt that full title.

"Quite well, thank you," the older of the two had demurely replied to this altogether formal, though gentlemanly form of address.

"May I present my cousin, Marshall Porter. Marshall, this is Miss Bailey of Wilberton. I believe you have heard of her father's famous studfarm."

"Ah yes," Marshall had said. "Delighted to make your acquaintance."

He had bowed and Ann had dropped him a sweet curtsy. He was charmed by the warmth of her smile, her porcelain skin and he noted with interest the frank gaze of her bright blue eyes.

"May I also present her sister, Miss Margaret Bailey."

Margaret had also dropped a curtsy. With light brown hair, a cupid bow mouth and green eyes, lustrous in the sunset glow of this summer's evening, Marshall thought she was very pretty indeed.

These Bailey girls would make perfect company. He and Richard could walk out with them as a four-some, perhaps take them for carriage rides. What a good way to spend one's time! Without a moment to lose he was already setting these delightful plans in motion.

"Perhaps we might accompany you for a short while this evening?" he suggested.

"That would be most kind," said Ann, "if you are in agreement, my dear sister."

Margaret had readily assented to this proposition.

"Our father has given us permission to stay at the fair for one hour. He has business to attend to."

"One hour!" Marshall had exclaimed, and then, mustering up as much gallantry as he could, he smoothly said, "Now, an hour well spent in the company of two pretty girls is more than Richard or I had ever dreamed of. This is indeed a rare and wondrous treat."

Both girls had been noticeably flattered. Ann had actually blushed, always a good sign! And Margaret had flashed him a smile which could not have been mistaken for anything but encouragement. Having learnt early in his life how to please his mother by his winsome ways, he was well practised in the art of charming the ladies.

"Richard and I have just had our fortunes told."

Ann had immediately given her opinion, "Oh dear! I should not like that at all!"

"Why not? It was very enjoyable, isn't that so, Richard?"

"Interesting, at any rate!" was Richard's brief reply.

"I think that we can only enjoy every day if the things that come are new and unexpected," Ann qualified her opinion.

"Agreed!" Marshall had heartily said, and added, cleverly using her words, "Meeting you both is an unexpected pleasure."

"What would be the value of knowing in advance what each day was to bring?" she went on. "One would never strive for anything. There could be nothing but futile longing, and yearning for the unattainable. There would be no ambition, no long-term plans for the future."

"Well said!" Marshall had been impressed. Here was a girl who was not afraid to speak her mind.

Now standing waiting to welcome the last of the guests to Wilberton Parish church, Marshall, with a sudden pang of realisation, remembered the old fortune teller's words: "I see family divisions!" How right she had been. Perhaps she could see into the future after all. He tried to recall the exact words of the riddles she had chanted: something about gaining his heart's desire and Richard losing his heart's desire. He now recognised that one of those was indeed true.

Reverend Merryweather, all smiles and patrimonial bonhomie, came up to him, patting him on the shoulder.

"Nearly time, I think. If one can trust the church clock, the bride should be here in five minutes. Quite a day! Glorious day for the bride! Difficult day for the bridegroom!" With a flourish of his hand and another smile, he moved off in the direction of some of his parishioners who had been invited to the Bailey wedding. Reverend Merryweather had never understood what had taken Richard Bailey, along with Ann and Margaret, away from his parish church for those eight years, and had never known what had brought him and his daughters back again just three months ago. This switch of allegiance, added to their sporadic attendance at his church, led him to secretly think the Baileys were a rather volatile lot.

Marshall's mind was still focused on the insurmountable problem between himself and Richard. He tried to remember when it had all gone wrong. One day Richard had been such good fun, and the next he was no fun at all: always working, helping Uncle Henry, and taking life far too seriously.

Cousin Charles had been much more fun! Together, over the past four years or so, they had travelled the length and breadth of the Fens, on horseback.

"What do you say we take the horses across Adventurers' Fen today and do a spot of duck-shooting?" Charles would have said, or "What do you say we ride over to Coveney and call on Aunt Martha and Uncle Robert?" or "What do you say we visit Mr Bailey and see the stud horses?"

He had always said an eager "yes" to a visit to the Baileys. Mr Bailey seemed to be pleased to encourage Charles in his chosen career as horse-doctor and, while the two of them toured the stables, Marshall had enjoyed the company of the two Bailey girls: Ann would sometimes play the piano for him, and Margaret would sing. Over the years a friendly relationship, perhaps a little more than that, had developed.

Richard now came out of the church, having dealt with Grandmother satisfactorily, in order to shake hands with other wedding guests and usher them to their pews. Now there will be trouble, thought Marshall. He imagined there would be a repeat of their last encounter when Richard had called him a "blackguard" and a "thief"! Such strange behaviour, he had thought at the time.

Apparently, Charles had been discussing their visits to the Baileys, now a weekly affair, and Richard had come riding over to *Hillrow Farm*, unappeasably angry, demanding to see him.

"Nothing short of a blackguard and a thief!" he had shouted. "You knew of my admiration for Ann Bailey. I made no secret of it! And you go behind my back. Oh yes. Charles has told me all: the musical afternoons, the walks in the garden, the moments alone! And you have known all along that I aim to marry her."

"You are mistaken, Richard," he had said, trying to be as calm as he could in this awkward situation. "I had no idea. Marriage? Does she know your intentions? You have never even paid court to her, that I am aware of!"

"I meet her every Sunday after church!" Richard had countered.

"You do not seriously think that polite conversation after church is courtship!" Marshall could not restrain his contempt for his cousin's lack of awareness of the way women should be treated. Polite conversation! No one could have construed that Richard had matrimonial designs on Ann Bailey. "You call me 'thief'? I cannot steal from you what is not yours. I demand that you withdraw this unjust charge."

Richard had refused, and that was the end of it. Since then, theirs had been an uneasy relationship, meeting only when absolutely unavoidable, putting on some sort of act during each intervening Christmas, to keep up appearances and not upset their respective parents.

Things between them had gone from bad to worse during the past few months. Mr Bailey had appeared to have no plans to attract Richard into the bosom of their family. Quite the contrary. It had been all too obvious to Marshall that Mr Bailey, under many pretexts, had encouraged him, and him alone, to court his elder daughter. Richard was not even in the running. Since the previous Christmas, there had been invitations to afternoon tea, to inspect the stud horses, to make up a dinner party, to escort Ann and her sister to Ely when they went in the carriage. Marshall knew that he was the intended husband for Ann. He had no objections. She was a lovely and lively girl, a fine pianoforte player, was not betrothed to anyone else, and above all was a rich man's daughter. She would do very nicely. So he had asked for her hand in marriage and she had accepted.

Reverend Merryweather was at his side again.

"I think you should go in now, sir, and take your place, for the bride and groom must not see each other before they stand before the altar of our Lord."

He patted Marshall on the shoulder again, gently pushing him in the right direction.

The congregation stood as the organist began to play the evocative opening bars of *Here Comes the Bride*, and Grandmother insisted that she be helped to her feet, even though her son Henry had suggested that she remain sitting.

"I may be doddery, Henry," she said, all too loudly, "but I am not incapable of standing at a wedding."

She saw her grandson, Marshall, in the front pew, and realised now for the first time whose wedding it was to be.

"He's a handsome lad. Always reminds me of your father. Lovely silky, fair hair."

Her son Henry gently squeezed his mother's arm. This was neither the time nor the place for reminiscences. She quietened down, only to start up again when Marshall turned round to look at the bride.

"I told you. He's a regular handsome lad. He'll break somebody's heart some day."

Marshall did not subscribe to the view that it was unlucky to turn round to catch a glimpse of the bride, though he did notice that Aunt Alice, serene and forbidding in her dark green brocade, looked at him more disapprovingly than she normally did.

Miss Ann Bailey, soon to be his wife, was truly a vision of beauty as she came slowly down the aisle on her father's arm. Marshall noticed that her long, wavy hair had been carefully coiffured into a chignon at the nape of her neck. Fine wisps of chestnut curls, interlaced with primroses, haloed Ann's fair face. He admired how the skirts of her ivory satin wedding gown swayed gracefully as she walked. He liked what he saw.

But he also noticed Mary Moody Rose standing tall beside his cousin Charles. She was a beauty! No pastel shades for Mary. She wore a scarlet dress, made of fine oriental silk specially imported. Her matching felt hat with its half veil of pink net, sat pertly on her head. She was looking directly at him, with an unmistakable twinkle in those bright blue eyes of hers. She could have been his for the taking. Marshall remembered how James Rose, Mary's father, had gone to great lengths to encourage their match, entertained him, had almost showered him with gifts and attention, but Mary was a strong-willed girl and had had her sights on Charles Porter from the beginning, and they were to be married the following year.

Looking back towards his bride, Marshall felt overall that he had made a wise decision to marry Ann. Her father had plenty of money to spare, the studfarm was a thriving business, and she had come with a dowry. This money had been spent all too quickly, he acknowledged that fact, but it had enabled him to take out a mortgage on a reasonably commodious four-roomed cottage at the other end of Main Street in Haddenham, much to the disappointment of Richard Bailey.

"I had hoped, my boy, that you and Ann would settle in the farm adjoining mine and we could have worked as a team. You know 'Richard Bailey and Son' has a good strong ring to it," he had sounded sad when he voiced his opinion to Marshall at the time.

"I will be close enough to give you a hand," Marshall had said.

Richard Bailey had noted the insincerity in the voice of his future son-in-law. He persisted anyway, "I am not getting any younger. I will need considerable help to keep the business from going under."

"Your business will continue to thrive," Marshall had dismissed the idea of the studfarm floundering. "People will always want horses. And you can get any number of stable lads to help you."

That had been all there was to the conversation. Richard Bailey could not understand how this young man could walk away from an opportunity to be partners in a business; but Marshall, having been long barred from the responsibilities of working with his father in his diversified farming concerns, was now demotivated. He had no intention of living in Wilberton, because to be too near his father-in-law would have meant helping out on the studfarm, and work was something to which Marshall was not particularly partial. Anyway, he had his allowance from his father.

As he watched Ann come slowly towards him, he could not help but notice that her hand did not simply rest on her father's arm: she clutched his arm instead, and her knuckles were white. He hoped that this tension was due to the natural apprehension and nervousness that he assumed any girl would feel on her wedding day. But then, as she reached the pew where Richard sat, she slightly turned her head in his direction. It was an almost imperceptible movement, but there was no mistaking her wistful, lost look, even through the veil. There was also no mistaking Richard's mirroring body tension and his regretful expression, as he exchanged with Ann an altogether too meaningful glance, fleeting though it may have been.

Marshall cast all of these observations aside, for Ann was to be his. After all, she had readily agreed to marry him, once her father had put before her the advantages of the match. In addition, although it had not been the original intention to outshine his cousin Richard, he now enjoyed this victory with relish and a sense of superiority.

The moment came for Marshall to join hands with his lovely bride before Reverend Merryweather.

"Dearly Beloved, we are gathered together in the sight of God..."

The ceremony had begun.

Despite his one or two misgivings, Mr Bailey did feel proud on this day: he was giving his daughter away to none less than a Porter, and the one with the finest prospects of wealth and social position. Not only did he look forward to basking in the glory of being related to the Porters after this event, but he savoured the fact that his future son-in-law, Marshall, would one day inherit all the Hillrow estate.

Richard Bailey was no fool when it came to business, and, with no sons of his own, he had begun to nurture two future sons-in-law, Marshall Porter was one and he had hoped that Charles Porter would be the other, as potential equal partners in the studfarm. It had been all too clear where Ann's heart really lay, but there was no room for sentimentality when it came to getting his daughters married, and when it came to business.

It was true that he had seen Ann with Richard Porter after morning service nearly every Sunday, exchanging pleasantries, sometimes standing a little more closely to one another than protocol or custom decreed. Richard Bailey found it puzzling that Richard had made no requests to court his daughter.

He had thought to encourage both Richard and Charles Porter as suitors for his girls, that was until he overheard a conversation in *The Rose and Crown* one evening the previous December.

James Rose, of Rose Villa, as the wealthiest shop-keeper in the village, and also as a father of four, was almost obsessed with the topic of inheritance and things material. He and his unmarried cousin, who had come down from Ely to share Christmas with him and his wife and family, were enjoying a pint of steaming ale in the snug.

"I can't say I approve, Kaleb," he was saying. "The larger the property, the bigger the profit. Once you divide it up in your will, then each of your beneficiaries has to start all over again. It's like slow financial suicide."

Kaleb was defending this new, more progressive approach to inheritance. "No, I say that it does each child good to know what is in store for him. It stops any jealousies. Don't you remember the terrible fights that happened after Great Uncle Bertram died?"

"But that was a shop. You can't divide a shop! This is different, I tell you. Henry Porter has made no secret of the fact that he is apportioning each of his children a certain amount of his property and his various enterprises. In this day and age, I predict that not one of Henry's family will have enough money to support a family on with the small amount they inherit."

"What about your daughter, Mary? There's a case in point! Her intended husband, Charles Porter will at least

82

inherit something. So she will have some security. With your system, her man would inherit nothing, and he'd have to lose face and work for his older brother, or work for you, and you have your own sons to consider." Kaleb reckoned he had won this argument, hands down.

"Now, I don't say that Mary won't benefit. Charles will inherit *The Red Lion Inn*. That's his share. And the older brother, Richard, will have *The Maltings*. But on principle, and I am talking principles here, it's not good policy."

There it was, the talk of the village: Richard, even though he was the eldest of Henry Porter's children, would have to share what was his birthright with his brothers and sisters! And Charles was to marry Mary Moody Rose.

Richard Bailey had lost no time in speaking to his daughters. "Ann, Margaret. Listen carefully. I have something I wish you to hear," he had solemnly commanded one evening late last autumn.

"Yes, Papa," they had both looked at their father inquiringly, for he rarely spoke to them quite so decisively at the dinner table.

"From now on we shall be attending Wilberton Parish Church," he obviously expected no discussion on the matter. His mind was made up.

Perplexed and more than a trifle upset at the prospect of not being able to see her Richard on Sundays after morning service, a meeting she looked forward to all week with a fluttering heart and hopes for the future, Ann whispered, "If you say so, Papa, but may I ask why the change of mind? We have grown accustomed to worship in Haddenham each Sunday."

Margaret understood her sister's feelings, but there was little she could offer to help in the situation, so she said nothing. As yet, she had no beau, Porter or otherwise, and she was as likely to marry someone who attended Wilberton Parish church as Haddenham parish church.

Richard Bailey simply said, "It is what I wish, and I am sure your poor dead mother would wish it too."

He then had switched his attentions to William Porter's family to supply a future son-in-law for his eldest daughter, for it was tacitly understood in the village that William Porter's eldest son, Marshall, would inherit all. Certainly, Marshall always behaved with the assurance and aplomb of a future landowner; a young man who had money to spend, but never seemed to need to work.

On this wedding day in Wilberton church, the silence, which followed the exhortation to any man in the congregation to "speak now or forever hold his peace", was interminable. Marshall feared that his cousin would shout out, "He's a blackguard and a thief!" and the wedding would be put off. Ann for her part longed to hear Richard speak out, but he did not.

It was very final when Reverend Merryweather loudly ordered, "Those whom God hath joined together, let no man put asunder."

Marshall and Ann were man and wife.

It may be said that Aunt Catherine was beside herself. Marshall knew that she would be emotional: it was ever her way. It would have been difficult, however, for an observer to determine whether she was at a wedding or a funeral, so freely were her tears flowing. She sniffed and sobbed, sobbed and sniffed throughout most of the proceedings, much to the annoyance of her husband.

William, as was often the case, experienced two polarised emotions: he wanted desperately to sympathise with his wife's genuine distress about losing a son, but deep down he was glad that the day had finally come when he would no longer have to share his house with that eldest son of theirs, who appeared to be constantly vying for Catherine's attention. He had encouraged the match between Marshall and Ann with a readiness all too transparent.

The words of the closing hymn, *Light Shining Out of Darkness*, were sung loud and clear by the congregation,

"*Judge not the Lord by feeble sense,*
But trust him for his grace;
Behind a frowning providence,
He hides a smiling face."

They were understood by all, except one, to mean that God had smiled on Marshall and Ann, bringing happiness to the young married couple on this their special day.

To the one in the congregation, there was *no smiling face*, simply *a frowning providence* which was hard to bear. Richard mocked himself ruefully as he tried to sing these words. He remembered that this was the hymn which had meant so much on that first day, when he had seen Ann Bailey in Holy Trinity church all those years ago. Now, as Ann stood before the altar of God, newly married to Marshall, the words took on an altogether different meaning.

God knows, over these past eight years, he could not have worked harder to be a worthy husband. He had increased production in the brewery, he had developed *The Maltings*, and he had introduced sugar-beet farming out at Linden End farm. He had saved his money wisely, he was becoming a rich man in his own right, and he was well respected in the community. He was ready. He had been literally on the verge of asking for Ann's hand in marriage, and entering a new life of matrimonial bliss.

Then Ann had stopped coming to Holy Trinity and within two months was betrothed to Marshall. It was a shocking blow. It had taken Ann away from him, Ann who was the reason for his existence and endeavours.

Moreover, it had divided him from Marshall.

"Family divisions"! The fortune-tellers had been right.

Marshall and Ann walked buoyantly up the aisle as man and wife. Both were smiling this way and that at their now joint families. Marshall could not resist a smile at Richard: a smile of triumph. His enjoyment of the moment, however, was only temporary, for he noted how Richard had the look of a man standing on the abyss of despondency. For a second he was filled with a sense of sorrow or guilt, as he remembered all of Richard's past kindnesses to him, and all the fun they had experienced in each other's company over the years. Perhaps Richard should have won the fair princess after all! But this was no fairy story: this was real life. In a flash he vividly recalled their last heated and hurtful exchange, and continued his smile. Richard may have felt betrayed: yet in truth, if he had wanted the girl, he should have spoken out. Like all girls, she was there for the taking!

He continued up the aisle smiling meaningfully at his past conquests, and raised an eyebrow at Mary Rose, the scarlet beauty. He winked at his young cousins from *Vine House*, though his twenty-year-old cousin Ann looked as disparagingly at him as Aunt Alice had done. Like mother, like daughter, he thought. He pulled a funny face at his younger brothers and sisters, thankful that he would no longer have to share in their antics. He was more than thankful too to escape the daily friction between his father and himself.

He could hear Grandmother following somewhere behind him saying,

"He'll break some young girl's heart some day!"

Although she was tittering at what was meant as a silly complimentary comment, unaccountably, Marshall suddenly felt party to a premonition. He had stopped smiling by the time he passed the christening font: he looked with distaste at the ugly, sculptured gargoyles surrounding the bowl. How could anyone have their babies baptised there? It was almost obscene, an insult to young humanity. He could now understand why his parents did not hold much store by christenings. Had they had the inclination to chat, on this point Marshall and his father would have found some common ground.

Then it was out onto the porch and into the springtime, with the sunlight filtering through pink cherry blossom. The nuptial celebrations were about to begin.

People were surrounding them, shaking him by the hand. Even his father shook him by the hand and patted him on the back, gruffly wishing him "good luck"; Ann was being kissed on the cheek by her relations, and then it was his mother's turn; Grandmother was standing close to him whispering something about "silky hair, just like your grandfather"; Richard Bailey warmly embraced him as his son-in-law; his mother came rushing girlishly over to him, still tearful, and told him "our doors are always open, my dearest boy," before she was adroitly whisked away by his father; and in a distant group, talking to his pretty fourteen-year-old cousin, Suzanna, was Richard. The third person in that group was a lithe, willowy and strikingly beautiful red-head: presumably this was Frances, Suzanna's school-friend from the seminary in Cambridge which they both attended. Then, Richard looked over towards him, and raised his top-hat.

Was it an attempt to be civil? Was it his way of healing the rift? Marshall thought a handshake would have been more appropriate. He nodded his head in return, and got back to the enjoyment of being the centre of the day's attention, with Ann by his side.

And then he realised that Richard had been raising his hat to Ann.

A cloud passed across the spring sun, and the noon air turned chill, as winter showed that he still had hold, and would not succumb to the warmth of the summer without a fight.

Chapter 5

RICHARD

April 2nd 1851

Richard lay beside Frances, as the early morning sunlight streamed through the square glass panes of their bedroom window. His heart missed a beat as he looked at her. He never failed to be amazed at the sheer brilliance of her red hair, a voluminous melange of fine copper wire, threads of gold and chestnut coils.

"Richard, never marry a redhead!" Not given to tact, Bill, on his own wedding day, had given his older brother advice, as the two of them had stood side by side at the front of Wilberton Church awaiting the bride. Bill was about to make his marriage vows to Margaret Bailey, Richard was his best man, and Ann, as Margaret's only sister, was to be matron of honour.

"What do you have against redheads?" Richard had asked, though the discerning ear would have detected a slight defensive coolness in the question.

Richard had talked and walked with Miss Frances Beales of Cambridge, when she had visited *Vine House* each Easter as the guest of their sister, Suzanna, but as the two girls were so much younger than Richard, Bill had not even suspected that his brother had any ulterior motives in keeping Suzanna and her redheaded friend company.

Bill blithely had given his opinion, clichéd though it was, "You know what they say! A redhead has a red fiery temper to go with it. One's life would be a misery! No, go for someone like Bailey stock with brown hair, like my Maggie."

Richard's sudden intake of breath and the straightening of his broad shoulders was answer enough for Bill.

"Sorry, Richard," Bill had muttered, realising his gaffe, "I didn't mean to bring that up again. But, come on, it's water under the bridge. Time to forget, eh?" Then he added, with serious circumspection, "It's always the best policy."

"Be assured, all is forgotten," Richard had not wanted any more family friction to spoil Bill's day, and he had even sounded comfortably resigned.

Caught up in his own concerns, Bill had genuinely forgotten about the family saga of Richard and Ann and Marshall, the love triangle of six years earlier, which had divided the two Porter cousins. He was doing the decent thing by tying the knot with the heavily pregnant Margaret. Now he shook himself free of the family scandal, his own worries and misgivings, and gave voice to a happy idea.

"I consider that today my marriage to Margaret will be the beginning of a reconciliation between you and Marshall: you know, two sisters marrying two cousins, cementing relationships; you will be able to meet Ann as the sister of my wife.

But Richard had not been thinking about Ann; Ann resided somewhere in a quiet sub-conscious corner of his mind, from where painful memories could not extrude.

He had been thinking of Frances. Frances, with her profusion of rich-red hair, filled his waking thoughts: lovely Frances, his quiet, refined and educated city-girl, for whom he felt an overpowering physical desire.

Now after four years of marriage, it was still true: Frances set his heart alight every time he laid eyes on her and every time he touched her. As she slumbered beside him, he gently ran the fingers of his left hand across her pale forehead, down her cheek and neck, feeling the silk of the skin under her chin, and, almost holding his breath, he lovingly caressed the soft contours of her breasts. He watched her face as she opened her eyes to this new day and to him.

"My dearest Fran," he said, using this diminutive name for her, as he always did in their quiet moments together. "Are you well this morning?"

"Much better, I believe," she replied, sounding much more cheerful than she had for weeks.

Since the birth of Henry Francis, their second son six months ago, she had been suffering from what the physician labelled anaemia, and had been so weak that they had had to employ a nursemaid to attend to the baby and to look after two-year-old Alfred Edward. Although Rebecca Powers was only thirteen, she had proved to be a worthy nursemaid, and as the daughter of a poor journeyman from Wilberton, she believed that she was the luckiest girl alive to have secured such enviable employment in such a well-to-do household.

"Doctor Hornbill's tonic must have done you some good!" Richard smiled as he spoke.

Frances nodded, for she did indeed feel more like her old self, and she was glad that she had agreed to see the doctor a fortnight ago. Of course, Doctor Hornbill had also insisted that she eat more meat, and drink at least two pints of beef tea per day; so, whether his tonic or the iron in her diet was responsible for her improvement was difficult to assess.

"Much better to seek expert advice, I say." Richard was reinforcing a point made a few weeks ago after his well-meaning Aunt Catherine had come to their house in Main Street, with some purple liquid in a corrugated glass bottle, labelled *Doctor Pott's Elixir of Life*. Frances had agreed to dose herself with this wondrous remedy, only to find that it had no effect whatsoever. "No more mountebank's preparations from now on, no matter who offers them," he finally said, as he sat up and placed his two feet on the soft Turkish rug beside the bed, as a prelude to getting ready for the important day ahead.

"Do you remember what today is?" he asked.

"This is the day of the census," she replied.

Carefully selected enumerators all over the country were getting ready this morning to record every single inhabitant of their designated local areas. Throughout the British Isles, the people were to be counted, for this was the day of the ten-year census, and Richard, as a well-respected pillar of the community and treasurer at Holy Trinity, had been appointed as the official enumerator for the parish of Haddenham.

"That's right," he said, proud of the part he was to play in this recording process.

Frances watched him as he walked across to the window. His muscular body was silhouetted against the early morning light. She sighed deeply. How she loved this husband of hers! And for the first time for many months, she felt a longing to be locked in his strong embrace; she once again yearned to feel his beautiful body close to hers, as they made love. She experienced a tingling in her breasts and an unquenchable fire inside her; she extended her right arm to him.

"Richard," she called softly, "come to me, my darling."

How his heart thrilled to hear these words, after the few months of self-imposed celibacy, during which time he had never once imposed his sexual desires upon her. Desperate months they may have been, but he was a man who would never take advantage of the weak or vulnerable.

Another April: another dawn. After the rich pinks of the sunset the night before, the young sun slanted through the shimmering swathes of fast-evaporating early morning mist across the fenland around Haddenham. There was a spring in the step of the farm labourers as they went to work on Richard's thriving fruit-farm at Linden End, where gooseberry and strawberry crops had been added to the successfully established sugar-beet yields. Others made their way to work on Thomas Granger's farm at Froize End, a huge hundred and sixty-four acre farm, which supplied vegetables and fruit to the ever expanding factories in Histon, where jams and other preserves were made. These men and women were confident that it was one of those special spring days, which acts as the vanguard of a warm and honeyed summer. They could almost hear, as a reality, the jangling of future coins in their pockets at the end of a successful season, bonuses from these two beneficent employers.

Today was no ordinary day.

It was a new beginning for Richard and Frances.

"More, Papa, more!" Alfred shouted with glee. Richard was energetically pushing him backwards and forwards on the nursery rocking horse, a treat which only his father bestowed on him. Rebecca was a little nervous of this fashionable toy, which had been bought in Cambridge and sent by special delivery in time for Alfred's second birthday the previous November. Having had little exposure to anything mechanical, she called it "that devilish contraption" and was terrified that her young charge would fall off and hurt himself, or worse still would get his little legs entangled in the squeaking metal hinges, or even hang himself in the red leather reins.

"Come on, little Frank, let's get you all lovely for Mama," Rebecca was gently cooing as she tended to Henry Francis, changing his clothing prior to taking him in to the mistress, who, despite her malaise, had insisted that she continue to breast feed her baby. Rebecca was a homespun girl, not given to frills and foppery, and she liked to call the baby Frank: Henry Francis seemed to be too big a mouthful for such a little mite! So Frank he had become.

Before Richard set off on this important day, he saw that Frances was sitting comfortably in her nursing chair in the bedroom. Elizabeth Chapman, their efficient housekeeper, had already set Frances's breakfast tray and an unopened letter on the mahogany table beside her.

"Ah, I know that unmistakable hand," he said, instantly recognising the flamboyant, sprawling writing on the manila envelope. There had hardly been enough remaining space to affix the Penny Black postage stamp!

"Yes. Miss Sharpe."

"The lady with the French poodle and the rings." Although Richard was laughing as he said this, his tone suggested a mild degree of censure. He recalled visiting this figure of artificial refinement, when he was courting Frances. Miss Sharpe, her old music teacher from Cambridge, was a pleasant enough individual, but her love of all things material and her gossip-mongering were distasteful to Richard's own sensibilities. However, her saving grace in his estimation was her sensitivity when it came to playing the pianoforte.

"You do not approve much of her, do you, Richard?"

"I would not put my opinion quite so strongly, my dearest. But try not to take everything she says too much to heart," he warned. He was acutely aware that, despite living in a grand, twenty-roomed town house with a modern mansard roof, Frances often felt claustrophobic in Haddenham village, after the bright city lights of Cambridge. Miss Sharpe's letters always heralded a bout of restlessness in his young wife.

Before he set off on this important day, he sat at his study desk, and opened the official census record book, a weighty leather-backed bound volume of stiff, ivory paper. In his fine copper-plate handwriting he had made the first entry:

"No 9 Main Street: Richard Porter, aged 35, brewer etc., born Haddenham."

After he had written these first words, he paused, with his quill pen poised in mid-air. He imagined what it must have been like to have been one of William the Conqueror's scribes, who were commissioned to compile records for the *Domesday Book*, the very first census in England. Perhaps they felt just as he did today: a sense of being part of something big. These records were for Queen Victoria to peruse, for politicians to draw conclusions from, for sociologists to pore over population trends and shifts, and for future generations to use in genealogy studies.

Even though he was aware of all of the ramifications behind these 1851 census returns, and of how important it was to record all the relevant facts, his own modesty would not permit him to record all that he himself was: namely, brewer, director of *The Maltings*, and fruit-farmer at Linden End. So he had written "brewer etc", to cover all.

Underneath, he had written,

Frances Porter, aged 24, wife, born Cambridge.
Alfred Edward, aged 2, son, born Haddenham.
Henry Francis, aged 6m, son, born Haddenham.
Elizabeth Chapman, aged 18, servant, born Wilburton.
Rebecca Powers, aged 13, nurse-maid, born Wilburton.

He had to remember to use the new, fixed spelling of Wilburton, in the census and not make any mistakes!

By the time Simon Stokes brought the immaculate, navy-blue carriage from the stables and coach house at the back of the property, round to the front door, Richard was ready and waiting, armed with his walnut writing case and the official census ledger. Yes, he felt a surge of pride as he donned his top-hat and descended the sand-stone steps of Number 9 Main Street.

"Good morning, Stokes," he said to this last of the Stokes brothers who followed in the family tradition of Porter coachmen and stablemen.

"Good morning, Mr Porter, sir! This is a big day, sir. Where do we start?"

"We'll start down at Froize End, right at the far end, work our way up to Linden End, and then we can have a rest at *The Cherry Tree*. After that, the left side of Main Street as far as my uncle's."

"I'll be glad to catch up on my brother's news. He and Clara have got four bonny girls now, you know."

"You can have a long stop there. I'll proceed on foot as far as the Green. The houses are so close together, that it would not be worth getting in and out of the carriage. But be sure to collect me at the Green at eleven o'clock sharp."

"Yes, sir. I'll be waiting for you. I can get the horses watered at the pond there."

"Good, for we have a long journey out to the other end of Hillrow by one o'clock. Then back to have lunch at *Vine House*." Richard had his itinerary well planned. "You can spend time there with your brother, John. He'll be pleased to see you."

"Thank you, sir. What with us all living our separate lives, I hardly ever have time to speak to him nowadays. Today's a regular treat for me."

"Good. You can get the horses fed there. In the afternoon it's out towards Haddenham End, then back down the right side of Main Street to finish off the day. Now, I think we are ready. So, let us begin."

"Yes, sir," said young Simon Stokes as he swung himself up onto the coachman's seat. He shook the reins as a command signal to the two waiting bays, and the day's enterprise was properly under way.

As Richard sat back in the carriage, he was filled with excitement for all that the day would entail, but there was a tinge of apprehension regarding one of his visits: he would have to call at the home of Marshall and Ann.

Richard was glad of the rest at *The Cherry Tree*, a tavern in Duck Lane at Linden End, set in the midst of a cherry orchard. He was pressed to partake of the daytime non-alcoholic speciality of a cup of warm milk flavoured with sugar and ginger. The morning had been more difficult than he had suspected. He had not been entirely satisfied with the veracity or validity of some of the entries in his census. Many of the good people in the outlying cottages out at Froize End were unsure of the exact ages of the occupants in their household, and some of them even had difficulty with their own date of birth.

"Let me see now. He would have been about twenty-four at the time of the cholera outbreak in Ely," said old Jubilee Wray about her son, Basil, who was up at Mr Granger's strawberry plantation pricking out young plants for next year's crop. "When was that, sir?"

Richard's knowledge of local history was being stretched to the limits, but he did know there had been two major outbreaks of cholera in that city.

"There was one in 1832 and one in 1837," he said.

"My sums never was any good. What does that make him then?"

"Let's see," Richard had patiently started to do his mental arithmetic, "that would make him either thirty-eight or forty-three."

"He were born when I were about thirty, I think. I was born on old King George's Silver Jubilee. That's how I was named Jubilee, on account of the king. Now when was that?"

Richard heartily wished he had brought with him a history book to help him out.

"That makes you seventy," he said, quite amazed that the dates of kings and queens, which Miss Arber had pumped into him at school, had remained intact.

"Well, I gave birth to my Basil when I were thirty, as I said, so what does that make him then?"

Although the sums did not quite add up, it seemed the more likely that Basil was thirty-eight, rather than forty-three, so "aged 38" was entered in the census. And there was no way of knowing if this was right or wrong, as Basil had not been baptised at the time; and there was no time to chase up other avenues to cross-check.

He now sat with his mug of steaming ginger-milk, musing over the possibility – no, probability – that the *Domesday Book* was not as factually accurate as the historians would have us believe.

His thoughts were interrupted by Peter Clay. "They say you be the numberumberator today. Is that so?"

"Yes, indeed, Peter, I am the enumerator," Richard replied, being particularly careful over his pronunciation.

"Beg pardon, sir, it's them long words. I can never get my teeth round them."

"No harm done, Peter."

"What do you have to do, if you don't mind me being so bold as to ask?"

"I write down everybody's name, age and occupation, and where they were born. It all goes into this big book."

"Would you mind if I was to see into that book. I can't read, mind, but I likes to see the letters crawl over the page like spiders."

Richard opened the book for him at a completed page.

Peter Clay whistled in admiration. "Like I said, little spiders crawling across the page. Jules, come over and have a look at this here writing."

Before Richard knew it, he was surrounded by a sea of old faces. It was definitely time to move on, and he closed the book and wished them all a very good-day and escaped into the bright mid-morning sunshine. Simon, from his stool in the snuggery inglenook, had seen him leave, and was ready to take him onwards in the direction of his Uncle William's at the bottom end of Main Street.

When the doorbell sounded, Mary Read, the housemaid at number eight Main Street, dashed across the scullery, dusting the flour from her hands and divesting herself of her kitchen garb, and walked as fast as she dared in order to open the front door. Mary's duties ranged from stoking the household fires to skinning rabbits, and from cleaning the stone floors to preparing winter doves from Farmer Woolden's dovecote for the Sunday table.

Opening the door to visitors who wished to call upon Mrs Porter was one of her favourite duties, as she got to see at first hand the finery worn by the ladies of the parish. The new bustles, which were fast becoming fashionable, were especially fascinating to this young house-servant. She had heard about, but had never actually seen one of the wire frames, which these avant-garde ladies wore under their skirts. The one half of her mind whispered, "Very uncomfortable, I should imagine", but, countering that opinion, an inner voice said, "I want to wear clothes like these rich ladies, and I will, one day."

She was always a little overawed when it came to ushering fine gentlemen into Mr Porter's study, and consequently was a little too free with her bobs and curtsies to which Mr Porter always said with deliberation, "That will do, Mary", and his "Thank you" was uttered with such an air of finality and command that she was hard-pressed to get to the door quickly enough and reach the security of the vestibule.

Opening the door this morning to Richard, she spoke quite huskily, "Good morning, Mr Porter, sir," and she bobbed him a brief curtsy.

"Ah, Mary," he said, noting the fact that she was out of breath, "is your mistress about?" He wondered if she might be consumptive, a condition which seemed to afflict so many young people these days, and indeed her eyes did seem unnaturally bright.

If the truth were told, opening the door to Mr Richard Porter had taken her completely off-guard. She had always secretly admired this attractive man of means, and, seeing him standing on the doorstep had set her heart all of a flutter.

"She is in the parlour at present, sir, engaged in a-writing of her letters. May I take your coat and hat, sir?"

"Lead the way, Mary," Richard gently ordered, after these preliminaries had been attended to, "but let us take our time. No need to rush!"

Mary smiled at him and believed that, had circumstances been different, she could have had him all to herself. For hadn't he married a girl not much older than she was? He had such kindness in those brown eyes of his! How she envied Frances! Shaking herself back into the real world, Mary opened the parlour door.

Aunt Catherine was indeed busy at her bureau, pen in hand, apparently oblivious of the sound of the door bell, or her nephew's voice in the vestibule. She even appeared flustered as Mary announced his arrival.

"Richard, my dear, what a delightful surprise!" she said, as he gave her the customary peck on the cheek. Always gullible when it came to outward demonstrations of affection, even this form of pleasantry was like manna to her. As he began to move away, she pulled him close. "To what do I owe this visit?"

"My dear aunt," he said, extricating himself from his aunt's over-zealous, loving grasp on both his hands, "if you remember, this is the day of the census."

Immediately recollecting herself, she said, "Ah yes, to be sure, hence the huge official tome!" pointing to the census ledger which he had placed on the desk. "Please do sit down. Mary, will you be so good as to ask my daughters to join us, and will you bring in a tray of that Italian coffee."

Richard lowered himself into the maroon, studded armchair in the corner near the bookcase. This was Uncle William's favourite chair when he spent time in this room.

As Mary left, there was no stopping Aunt Catherine. "Now, Richard dear, you must tell me what you think of the coffee, when it comes. Mr Rose procured it for us. Normally, it would have cost us dear, but as he is a relation now, distant I know, he only charged us half price. How is dear Charles? Must be married ten years by now. Wasn't he married just after Marshall?"

"In the same year, certainly, but in the autumn, with the leaves falling all around us, you remember."

"Ah yes!" Aunt Catherine's expression changed to one of wistfulness. By the little, troubled lines which were furrowing her brow, Richard knew that she was thinking about Marshall, and her thoughts were far from happy ones. "We hear so little of him nowadays."

Richard was, for a moment, unsure of whom the pronoun "him" referred to, until she continued the question,

"Are he and Mary happy in Ely?" Even then, Richard, ever the sensitive listener, noted the slight emphasis on "he and Mary", and like an unwilling eaves-dropper, heard the sub-conscious comparison at work. Here they were, his aunt and he, talking pleasantries on the surface, with a lurking sub-text of worries and unspoken thoughts, but understood by both.

"Yes indeed, Aunt! Charles has all any man would desire. A fine wife, two healthy boys and two equally healthy girls, a solid business as a horse-doctor – a veterinary surgeon is what he is called these days." Richard could have bitten his tongue, for, by championing his brother whom he admired, he was adding fuel to the daily fire of dissatisfaction, which was felt towards Marshall in this house.

However, Aunt Catherine was off on another tack, a favourite topic of hers. "But Ely is so noisy, and I should hate to hear the cathedral bells and all the other church bells ringing incessantly. It would drive me quite distracted!"

Aunt Catherine was not a devout Christian: in fact, having insisted that she and Uncle William were married in a registry office, and not even having had all their children baptised, religion played a minimal role in her life.

There was a knock on the door and Richard's three female cousins entered the room. There was no mistaking or ignoring Edna: at twenty-five she was still a hefty girl, sturdy and dark-haired like her father, but her early fidgety behaviour had developed into a dynamism which the new thespians would call "stage-presence".

"Richard!" she cried, as she ran over to him. He liked her forthright approach, her genuine affability and her lack of pretentiousness. "So this is your big day... Richard the Scribe! I like that name for you. Important and historical at the same time!"

Mary and Rachel had sat down on the ottoman by the window, which looked out onto the street. They were gentle souls, not unlike their mother in looks with their fair hair and pale blue eyes. However, whereas Catherine exuded warmth and craved affection, these two girls appeared to be insipid and uncommunicative. They had both come of age, but Uncle William would not entertain the idea of them marrying before their elder sister, Edna, sometimes spelt "Ednor" in her more eccentric moments, had tied the matrimonial knot.

"How is dear Frances?" Mary ventured to enquire.

"Much improved, I am happy to say," he replied.

"You see, Edna. I knew *Doctor Pott's Elixir* would give her back her strength," Aunt Catherine said triumphantly, nodding her head.

Richard said nothing, but he could not avoid exchanging glances with Edna, who obviously shared his distrust of quack medicines.

Mary and Rachel had grown fond of Frances, and had genuinely tried, in their own little ways, to help her to settle into her new life in Haddenham. They had brought little posies of flowers to cheer her, they had sat with her as they worked at their tapestries; they had made quiet conversation about inconsequential things. Frances was a lover of the arts: music and literature. She was a modern, educated woman who could hold her own in any philosophical debate. Much as she appreciated the effort, which Richard's two young cousins were making, their paucity of thought convinced her that she did not belong in this village, or indeed any village. She envied Mary, her sister-in-law, whose husband Charles had taken her away from Haddenham, and she had said as much to Richard on a number of occasions.

"Have you heard the absolutely wonderful news?" Aunt Catherine was beginning to bubble with excitement as she pointed towards Edna, who had at last seated herself beside the occasional table near the marble fireplace. "Edna has met a young man. Thomas Jones, a farmer from Littleport. Such a common name, I'm afraid to say, but he is polite and gentlemanly, and he is most kind to Edna; and what is more, he has expectations. Your uncle and I have high hopes that the two of them will be married in the not too distant future."

"Mama, nothing is settled, you know." Edna tried to show some composure, in what was an unexpected divulging of information. She herself had "high hopes" that Thomas would ask for her hand in marriage, but she was not happy that it should almost be a foregone conclusion, or spread about, even to her favourite cousin.

Noting Edna's reticence and agitation, Richard put down his empty coffee cup and said, "Now, should we get down to the business of the day without further ado?"

"What information do you require?" said Aunt Catherine. So used to her husband taking control of her life, she was beginning to feel apprehensive. "I do hope we shall be fit to answer all your questions!"

"You make it sound like a police investigation! I do assure you, this is an entirely harmless process. I am no Robert Peel!"

He opened his book and his writing case with an air of officialdom, which somewhat belied his words. He had not intended to be ostentatious, but the ledger was uncommonly large, and his writing case did take some effort to open and set up in readiness to make the necessary entries.

Richard, of course, knew all of the details which he required about this household, but his brief was to visit each home and premises in person and gather information from the occupants.

He made a start and spoke out loud the words as he entered them:

"William Porter, aged 57, Farmer of 135 acres, born Haddenham."

"You had better write in that he has six labourers too. Now there's Samuel Thixton and—"

Richard was obliged to interrupt his aunt, "There's no need for those details. I just need the people who live here: family and employees."

"In that case, there's the house-servant, Mary Read. She lives here."

Richard wrote: *Mary Read, aged 19, house-servant, born Haddenham,* leaving six lines blank to insert the family names.

Then he made the entry for his aunt, sensitive to the fact that she was not keen to divulge her age at first:

Catherine Porter, aged 58, wife, born Rampton.

He got no further than writing the following entry: *Stephen Porter, aged 32, son, farmer, born Haddenham,* than Aunt Catherine, finding it impossible to give Richard the details he required without recourse to extraneous information, started to chat.

"I suppose you have heard that he is to go to America? His sights are set on developing a fruit farm in a place called Florida."

For as long as Richard could remember, Stephen had talked of the grand opportunities which awaited him in America. Yet he was still here! He did not voice that opinion, simply observing,

"He always had a love of America... even when he was a little boy."

"But why do you think he wishes to uproot himself? He can grow fruit here. And Florida is mosquito infested they say! He may die of that awful malaria disease. Some kind of swamp fever. It is just too dreadful."

"Mama, do not distress yourself," said Edna. "He has never been sick; illness just passes him by."

"But your father will miss him on the farm," she persisted.

"I doubt it," Edna could not resist this contradiction. "His head is so full of America that he has hardly been able to concentrate on any work here."

Both Stephen and Marshall in their different ways were a disappointment to Edna, who used to be so proud of her older brothers. She knew who helped run the farm with her father; she knew who had the energy and drive to face working alongside him; she knew who exuded a fierce sense of family pride.

"No, it's Knight who is the greatest support," she said simply. "If it was not for Knight, I do not think Papa could have built up the farm to its present size."

Aunt Catherine, with Stephen instantly supplanted by Knight as the foremost son in her thoughts, proudly announced, "Do you know, Richard, they have expanded into mangold-worzels, wheat and celery? And I hear Knight talking about setting up a flower bulb industry." Aunt Catherine's excitement was beginning to get the better of her. "It is so adventurous, don't you think?"

"The Dutch will have to beware!" Richard was not too sure about the requirement for flowers in the Fens, but he humoured his aunt, nevertheless.

He brought the conversation back to the day's task. "Now, let us get Knight's details written down."

Aunt Catherine dictated: *"William Knight Porter, aged 29, farmer, born Haddenham."* Then she was off again. "Next there is Henry and then Jacob."

Edna interrupted her mother, "Mama, only the people who live here, remember!"

"Ah yes. Wasn't it a pity that Henry and Jacob showed no interest in the farm and moved away? But Jacob does visit us every now and again, you know."

Richard agreed with his aunt, though he doubted if his two cousins would have been much use. Henry had planned to move up north from the time he was twelve, and, having done so, he presently enjoyed his role as manager of one of Blake's "satanic mills". Jacob, on the other hand, went south, never having been particularly interested in being a farmer: he always had his sights set on a busy city life in the midst of professional people, and had moved to London on his eighteenth birthday. He made occasional visits to his brother Knight's house, calling himself a "gentleman", over the next few years, but beyond that he was lost to his family.

The details of Edna, Mary and Rachel were entered in the census ledger, and Richard began to make ready to leave.

A chatterbox she may be, but Aunt Catherine had deliberately avoided any discussion of Marshall. She had her private reasons. The apple of her eye had proved to be cankerous after all, though she would never admit as much to her husband or to anyone. Her eldest son, her Adonis, had fallen from grace! She had succumbed to his charms time and again, when he wheedled and begged for money to satisfy his selfish lifestyle, but Marshall had wanted more and more. Finally, she could give no more to her fallen angel, without her husband suspecting.

She thought she now understood the reasons for the gulf which existed between her husband and their eldest son. She was wrong, of course! Marshall had sense enough not to ask his father for more than his customary allowance and what he was due for work done on the farm. The fact that Marshall had failed to prove himself hard-working, during his few hours on the farm each week, was hardly annoyance for a man who enjoyed the power of sole ownership and responsibility. Marshall's lifestyle as a dissipated gentleman of means, though the talk of the village, meant little to William. No, William's dislike of his son was based on jealousy, and nothing more, the seeds of which had been sown on that Christmas day nearly twenty years ago.

Richard had no wish to discuss Marshall, and his cousins had learned through bitter experience never to mention their brother Marshall within earshot of either their mother or their father, the former turning pale at the mention of his name, and the latter turning red!

So, Marshall remained a silent, yet all too pervasive, presence in the room.

Richard knew that, later in the day, he would have to call at Marshall and Ann's cottage at the far end of Main Street. He dreaded what lay in store.

Stokes, a stickler for precision when it came to time-keeping, was waiting at the Green, as promised, when the church bell sounded eleven o'clock.

Richard rounded the corner from Main Street, his writing case swinging by its hinged leather handle from his right hand, and the weighty book held firmly under his left arm. Half of the Haddenham census was now complete. It had not been as slow a process as he had at first feared. In the town, things had been more straightforward, simply because the shopkeepers and owners of the comfortable dwellings, which ran up Main Street, were more able to give Richard the information straight away, or had knowledge of where to find the written records, and, what's more, had been able to read them, or had written them out in readiness for his visit.

They set off down the long causeway towards Hillrow. The throbbing from Setchell's new flour mill, just set back from the Green, could be heard. It was an exciting sound, positive and strong. As the carriage rumbled along towards the few outlying houses and cottages at Hillrow, Richard had time to sit back and consider the changes which he was planning for himself and his family. He was convinced that steam power was the only way forward in this modern world, and, no matter how the purists and historians might rue the demise of the old ways, in business one could not remain static in this fast-moving world of industrial progress.

Richard had believed steam power should be introduced at the *Vine House* brewery and at *The Maltings*, but found that his ideas had fallen on deaf ears. His father, a maltster following in his father's footsteps, had been loath to adopt new ways.

"You're just like your Uncle William: jumping straight into new-fangled machines, just for the sake of them."

"Steam power is hardly new-fangled in this day and age," Richard had said the previous Christmas, over port and a cigar after their customary luncheon of roast goose. "Think how fast things are developing. Who knows what the inventors will have for us by the turn of the century? If we get left behind, then that will be the end of the brewery."

"This brewery has been in the family for over a hundred years. It has been successful all of that time. It will go on being so. There will be no changes made during my life-time." He had closed his mouth firmly. Then as an after-thought he added, "What you do with it after I am gone is your business."

Richard knew that his father would not change his mind. A kindly and sensible man in most spheres, but when it came to the brewery, his love of the family heritage blinded him to the serious threat that modernism posed. Richard's mother, that gritty breed of brewer who had reigned supreme, might once have taken Richard's part and moved with the times, but she now tended to agree with Aunt Catherine.

"All that pumping and hissing and throbbing would be quite intolerable. You remember how your Uncle William had to sell *Hillrow Farm* because your aunt could not tolerate the noise? We should have to sell *Vine House* and move away, you know. Is that what you want, son? It has been in the family for generations." Alice knew how to gain the advantage.

"That is not what I want," he had said, knowing that she had won the argument. He loved *Vine House*, and she knew it. *Vine House* should be his one day soon. Of course he did not want it to be sold.

Consequently, they were being overtaken by more progressive breweries, in nearby Ely. Richard could clearly see the writing on the wall, and knew that, before long, the local Porter brewing concerns would grind to a halt, resting on antiquated laurels which had no place in this modern age. It saddened him to see the family business "dwindle, peak and pine", and there was nothing he could do to persuade his father to modernise.

He was certain that, to create a successful, progressive brewery, he would have to buy premises elsewhere. In fact he

107

had already tentatively set the wheels in motion. Mr Symmonds, his agent in Ely, had informed him of premises in Bugg's Lane which he considered to be suitable and highly desirable". Richard was to go to Ely the following week to inspect these quality premises, named *The Eagle and Lamb,* and to discuss terms.

The carriage slowed as they approached *Hillrow Farm.* As details of the occupants were recorded, Richard specifically listened out for the so-called "distracting" noises emanating from the steam powered engine which had driven his aunt and uncle away, but there was only a little purring and gentle hissing to be heard. Richard wished his parents could hear for themselves, but he knew in his heart of hearts that they would not change their minds.

They went on to interview the Newell family who lived in one of the nearby cottages. Jeremiah Newell was a young man of twenty, who had an ambition to own his own plot of land, and each month he had put a little money, which he earned as a labourer at *Hillrow Farm,* into his grandmother's old brown teapot.

"Before you're dead and gone, Nan, I will take you walking across my bit of land. Newell land, it'll be," he would promise her, each time she asked him what he was putting into her bit of old crockery.

"That'll be nice, dear," she would say. "It 'ud better be soon, for I don't think I'm long for this world. And I don't want to be carried over it in my coffin, neither!"

By half-past one, Simon Stokes had pulled up in the coach-yard at the back of *Vine House,* and Richard was seated at the dining-room table with his mother and father, his sister Ann, and fifteen-year-old brother, Henry John.

Now, it must be recorded here that Henry John had come as a complete surprise to his middle-aged parents. With irregularities in her menstrual cycle, Alice had believed that her child-bearing days were over. She honestly had been of the opinion at the time that she was becoming "portly", and it was only when she had felt unmistakable movements inside her womb that she had realised that she was to have another child.

Richard's mother and father had gathered all the family round in the drawing room one fateful Sunday afternoon in late July.

"Your mother and I have something important to tell you," Henry had said, standing rather majestically behind his wife who sat on the chaise longue. She had taken his hand which rested on her shoulder, and derived from it some moral support for the news she was about to break.

"My dears, your father and I," she faltered momentarily, "your father and I are to have a 'love-child'."

This announcement had been met with a stunned silence. This mother of theirs was not the kind to have babies! She was a brewer, a strong-minded boss of thirty employees, a woman not given to outwardly feminine ways, not like Aunt Catherine who was always producing babies!

"Is not that delightful news?" Henry had asked, taken aback by his sons' and daughters' reception of this future addition to the family. He waited for some kind of response.

Richard, a mature nineteen-year-old at the time, had felt some slight degree of embarrassment, but mainly worried why his parents should want another baby at this time of their lives. He mulled over the consequences, which were bound to upset the cosy equilibrium that existed in *Vine House*.

"When is the baby due?" he had managed to ask, but was unable to say how pleased he was, for that would have been an untruth.

"We are not quite sure. Probably October," his mother had answered, but she had been aware of Richard's laboured question and lack of enthusiasm. She felt a little hurt by his reaction, for he was normally so kind and thoughtful. What she did not understand was that Richard was troubled by the awareness that home life would not be the same. He was faced with the realisation that *Vine House* could no longer be his when he married, for it would still be the family home of a growing child. He would have to wait until the child had become an adult. He would have to adjust to a new future, a new home. He had been at a loss to know what he could say to his parents on that summer's afternoon.

Suzanna hardly spoke. Her mother had hoped that she would enthusiastically hug her and be pleased at the prospect of a baby to cuddle and pet. However, Suzanna was used to being the baby of the family, loved by all, and she wondered how it could be "delightful news" to have her position usurped. Although she often insisted that she was grown up at seven years old, today she desperately wanted to be very young indeed!

Ann, normally so stiff and proper, had a tearful look about her, as if she had suffered some terrible disappointment. She was twelve years old, her body had matured and she knew that she could bear children now. She had been so proud of these new physical developments, and had talked to her mother about them. They had talked, woman to woman. Her mother had praised her and talked of the wonders of womanhood. And now, her mother seemed to have stolen the march on her, and had gone one better.

Misinterpreting the tears for those of pleasure, Alice said, "I knew you in particular would be very happy. Those are little drops of womanly happiness, are they not?"

Ann had nodded. What could she say?

Charles and Bill behaved rather badly on that day, for they had difficulty suppressing their incredulity. The notion that their parents could create a "love-child" was just too absurd. Surely they were too old for love!

At seventeen and fifteen respectively, Charles and Bill were the age for "love". Each would fantasise from time to time: now the hero of a tale of unrequited love, now Romeo beneath Juliet's balcony, now the saviour of a maiden in distress in some tale from long ago, now seduced by Sophia in the dark closet under the stairs, now a love-sick minstrel singing a lonesome ballad to his "mistress's eyebrow"! They also experienced some real enough stirrings of sexual arousal, especially when Ellen Timkins's fleshy bits were deliberately and saucily flaunted at them in Holy Trinity church.

All in all, that summer's afternoon in the *Vine House* drawing room had been too memorable to forget, and it had left its indelible mark on everyone.

Although he had brotherly feelings for Henry John, the "love-child" who had grown into a strapping and ambitious young man, Richard found it difficult to love this precocious boy. After all, Richard should now be living in *Vine House*: it had always been planned that he would move in here when he married. His parents should now be living in the accommodation next door, like Grandfather and Grandmother had done before. He, as the eldest son, and Frances, his wife, should be bringing up their sons in the Porter family home.

It was yet another bitter pill to swallow. In his bid to make something of his life, to make money, to extend his farming interests and to buy his own house, he had lost what he loved. First Ann, and now *Vine House*! Henry John, the young brother who had been spoiled throughout his life, had supplanted Richard. Henry John, loved above all others by his parents, would get what he wanted. Future family divisions cast their shadow, as Richard considered inheritance, and where Henry John fitted into the plans outlined so many years ago in the drawing room. Nothing had been said by their father about Henry John's portion of the Porter estate and concerns.

One cold certainty was that *Vine House* was not considered to be Richard's any more, now or in the future: his mother had even mentioned selling it, if he were to modernise the adjoining brewery. His parents had no intention of modernising the brewery, so his livelihood would be sure to quickly disappear. He had long ago determined to be one of the best brewers in Cambridgeshire. Mentally, he cemented the decision to buy the premises in Bugg's Lane in Ely, and there he would build one of the finest breweries in the county. More than that: he made up his mind, there and then, sitting round the luncheon table on this day of the census, to go to live in Ely. He would sell the land he owned outright, he would employ a manager to run the *Vine House* brewery, Henry John could take over the management of the Porter farmland, and he would forge his own future from now on.

Later in the drawing-room, Richard wrote the *Vine House* entry into his census ledger:

Henry Porter, aged 62, brewer and maltster, brick-maker and farmer, born Haddenham (170 acres, with 6 labourers)

Alice Porter, aged 60, wife, born Stretham.

Ann Porter, aged 27, daughter, born Haddenham.

Henry John Porter, aged 15, son, born Haddenham.

Sophia Penning, aged 19, servant, born Haddenham.

Those were the only names recorded, for the rest of the family had flown the nest.

Bill and Margaret still lived in Wilburton, where he would help his father-in-law with the running of the studfarm, in between his duties down at the Porter brick-making business. Truth to tell: neither of these concerns was blooming.

Where steam power would be the key to Richard's later prosperity as a brewer, it worked against the Bailey studfarm, for the advent of the steam train had meant fewer dray-horses were required across the county. Mr Bailey was getting too old to diversify, his older son-in-law Marshall had never once lent a hand on the farm, or even made suggestions for improvement or moving with the times. All he had been good for was getting money out of him on one false pretext after another, till there was precious little left to give. What a mistake he had made there! He worried for his daughter,

Ann, and her children. But all might be well, even so, once Marshall inherited his father's farm.

Bill, his younger son-in-law was a decent fellow, despite his earlier indiscretion, but he had his own concerns to see to, with responsibility for the brick-making business and the two clay pits out at Haddenham End.

Bill had suffered a huge disappointment when the plans submitted by Joseph Paxton for the building of The Crystal Palace were adopted. Paxton's amazing structure was to be made of iron and glass, regarded as a feat of modern engineering, and in many ways it was to surpass the contents of the Great Exhibition which were displayed therein. The exhibition's committee had originally submitted their own design: a building requiring some sixteen million bricks. Bill had been excited at the prospect of supplying a proportion of these bricks, perhaps four or five million, and growing rich in the process.

When these plans were cast aside in favour of the glass structure, now already erected in Hyde Park in readiness for the grand opening of the exhibition in May, Bill had decided that he would have to make a mark for himself in his life, and he would not depend on the whims of distant planning committees. He would go into business, for he did in fact have a "good business head on his shoulders", as his father had noted all those years ago, but his heart was in farming, for wasn't he of solid farming stock? Already it had been rumoured in the village that he and Margaret were thinking of going to America to fruit-farm, like cousin Stephen. The rumours on this occasion would prove to be right.

Little Suzanna, no longer the baby of the family would soon have a baby of her own. She had married Edward Mann, a good man from Soham, who had fallen for her natural grace and beauty, as well as her lively, educated mind. Suzanna had pressurised her mother and father, when she reached the age of fourteen, to such an extent that they had finally agreed to send her to Miss Michael's Seminary for Young Ladies. There she had gained four years instruction in all the "refinements which any modern woman should require in life", and where she also received comfortable board and lodging under the careful eye of Miss Caroline Michael herself.

Suzanna's time in the ladies seminary in Cambridge had served her well. It had served Richard well too, for he would not have met his own darling Frances, had it not been for Suzanna's determination to be educated in a good school for young ladies. It was on one of his last visits to Cambridge, to have afternoon tea with his sister in her apartment, that he had found himself alone with Miss Frances Beales. This was by no means a coincidental meeting. Suzanna, sensitive to her eldest brother's unhappiness at the time of Marshall and Ann's marriage, had finally decided that she would play match-maker. She knew that Richard and Frances liked each other and were well-suited, despite the age difference. It had been a happy day for Suzanna, when she had seen her favourite brother and her dearest friend married in St Giles Church in Cambridge. She had been proud to be their bridesmaid.

Ann, at twenty-seven, was fast becoming the proverbial "old maid", and although she played the piano well, and ran *Vine House* now, she was still a quietly cold and somewhat critical body, who tended to shun shows of affection. In consequence, those around her had learned to offer few. Besides, her parents lavished all their love and attention on young Henry John, so there appeared to be little room in their hearts for her. Hers was a lonely life in the midst of her family.

At the time of Suzanna and Edward's wedding, as the older sister, it had pained Ann deeply that she had been left behind in the matrimonial race. It embarrassed her that it should have been made so publicly obvious by the part she had to been asked to play. She and Richard had been witnesses at the wedding, and, although nothing but kindness

114

had been intended, she had felt the twist of the knife in the wound. It was a wound which was never to heal, as she embraced a future of spinsterdom.

Richard thought of Charles and Mary and their happy family, all now living in Ely. He imagined with pleasure how well Frances would settle in Ely with Mary as a friend. He inwardly nodded as he envisaged how he would enjoy living close to his brother, who as a publican shared the same interests. Yes, it was time to make a move, and he felt a surge of happiness and relief at the prospect. All of his worries for the future would be over, and Frances would be happy.

So here he was, at the very last house. The sky was a deep red, heralding another good morrow: the farmers would be already counting their blessings and their almost guaranteed harvest monies. Richard took a deep breath as he knocked on the simple wooden door of his cousin's cottage.

In his mind's eye he always somehow kept the image of Miss Ann Bailey, as she was, in Holy Trinity church on that Christmas day, when he had first set eyes upon her. Her chestnut curls, her porcelain skin, her smile to him.

Who can describe the guilt-ridden, heartfelt pain that pierced Richard's heart when Mrs Ann Porter opened the door to him on that April day? No maid to usher the visitor to the parlour, no help in housewifery duties, no nursemaid to help with the children. The sunset glow faded, as if in sympathy with the diminished lustre of her curly hair, which hung untidily round her shoulders, a parody of its former glory. She did not wear a lace cap, the norm for all married ladies in that part of the country. It was altogether rather unseemly, and sad.

"So, is this Matilda?" he managed to say, stroking the smooth down of the four-month-old baby whom Ann carried. He could not help but notice that Matilda was probably in mid-feed, for Ann's bodice had been hastily drawn across her breasts, revealing all too much to him, or to any visitor. He forced himself to look at the baby's pert, yet serene, little face, and added, "She's a pretty little thing." Sounding like his grandmother, he found himself, for some unaccountable reason, saying, "She'll break somebody's heart some day."

"Hello, Richard. I knew to see you sometime today, what with the census, but I expected you earlier." Then with an expression full of regret and full of yearning, "We could have had time to talk then."

He looked into her eyes, almost into her inner soul. What he wanted to say, what he had always wanted to say, were words to remain forever unspoken.

"And Priscilla," Richard said, thankfully noticing the five-year-old hiding in the grey skirts of her mother's faded dress, and clutching nervously to her mother's apron. Reminding himself yet again of his grandmother, he found himself telling a white lie, "What a lovely girl you are!" He was all too aware of the child's thin appearance. Aesthetes and artists might have been in raptures about the child's deep and sultry eyes: Richard thought this little girl looked undernourished.

An intemperate voice sounded from the room to the back of the cottage. "Come in, come in, whoever you are! Let's have a jar of ale and be merry!"

Ann tried to effect a smile, but her innermost feelings prevailed upon her facial features, so that all Richard saw was a sorrowing grimace.

"He's in the back parlour. I'll take you to him," she said dully.

"But how are you? Are you well?" Richard asked on the way down the darkening corridor, not wanting to hear what he feared, yet needing to know. Not that he could do anything to help. He had decided long ago that it was not possible to assist Ann in anything financial, without pouring more coals on an already roaring fire of discontent. No matter what his feelings, it was not his place to give money to another man's wife.

"You can see," she said. A simple and telling response! She opened the door for him and disappeared into the other room at the back of the cottage: hardly a nursery, thought Richard; but more likely a scullery or a bedroom.

Richard had suspected that Marshall would be inebriated, from the conversation he had accidentally overheard, when he had been in *The Plough*, taking down the particulars of the landlord and his family just half an hour earlier.

The Plough now belonged to the younger Metcalfes. As Richard had been writing their biblical names of *Joseph* and *Mary* in his book, followed by the names of their two girls, *Mary aged eight* and *Elizabeth aged five*, some local brickmakers had been discussing Marshall in the snuggery. It appeared that he had only just left.

"I don't know what's to become of 'im," Samuel Thaxter had pontificated, for all the world like an aging prelate. He was only forty-seven, but he had been giving his opinion to his twenty-five year old son, Charlie, whom he thought to be easily led, especially when it came to people offering free drinks. Seated beside Charlie was John Disboro, another brick-maker down at Haddenham End, an even more impressionable young man of eighteen years, so Samuel had wanted to sound more worldly-wise on purpose.

"He's all right," Charlie had disagreed, "always treats us fair: buys us many a jug of ale! Quite the gent, he is!"

"No. That's not the ways of gentlefolk," Samuel was quite adamant. "That's the ways of the likes of you and me. We buy any amount of drink for our friends, but how often do you catch the gentry dippin' their hands in their pockets for the likes of us, eh? Christmas and Easter, and the odd Goodening Day. That's all. And he's gentry. He may have forgot it, but don't you forget it, for he'll be the boss around here one day."

Undeterred, Charlie had continued, with a knowing nod and a wink to his young friend and work-mate, "I loves to hear his stories of all his shenanigans with his women friends!"

John had then pitched into the conversation, "That's right. Do you remember the one about him and young Jenny Tanner, down by Setchell's mill! What, with all that mighty throbbin' and puffin', it were very steamy!"

This piece of vitriolic gossip, disguised as coarse humour, had displeased Samuel. He did not want to hear any more. However, he had to agree that there were too many stories abounding about that young gentleman's behaviour, and that "there was no smoke without fire".

"He'll come to no good, you mark my words." He had spoken with an air of finality, and had sat back in his chair, knowing that he had brought the conversation to an end.

In the back parlour, Marshall was stretched out before a newly stoked fire, his shirt awry, his breeches undone. Young George, his ten-year old son, was ensconced in a corner reading an old and tattered book by the light of a candle. Neither cowardly nor shy, he was a patient child, who inherently believed in the least line of resistance. He said nothing, hoping to be unnoticed in the gloom.

"Ah, Cousin Richard!" Marshall slurred. "And to what do I owe this pleasure?" The heavy irony was not lost. Even young George became wide-eyed, wondering what would follow.

"Good evening, Marshall. You know why I am here. It's the day of the census."

"To be sure! To be sure! The government's messenger-boy!"

Desperately trying to avoid confrontation, Richard turned his attentions to young George. "And George, good to see you, young man. Quite the scholar, I see! Let's see your book." Examining the writing on the faded blue front cover, with the material fraying at the edges, he said with genuine interest, "Ah, *Robinson Crusoe*. One of our old favourites when we were your age."

He and Marshall exchanged a momentary look: a fleeting remembrance of Jessie in the *Vine House* nursery. The stories of adventure then were like gold promises of a glorious and magnificent future. How brave and strong and successful they would both be! Jessie had filled their young heads full of optimism.

Both Richard and Marshall had their own reasons for smiling ruefully.

Marshall expansively indicated the armchair on the other side of the hearth. "Well, sit down and have a jar! George, get your mother to fetch us some of the best ale!"

Richard said, as George obediently went on his errand, "He's a fine boy. Good to see a boy who likes reading."

Ignoring this as a common-place pleasantry, Marshall concentrated his thoughts on the reason why his cousin had deigned to visit him. "The day we are all to be counted, and put into categories, like some cattle or horses at a fair!"

"Just the names, ages and occupations," Richard kept cool, and answered quite factually.

"Do you know why they want all the names and ages and occupations?" Marshall deliberately enunciated each of those nouns clearly, poking his right index finger into the air with each one.

"Just the ten-year census," Richard replied, trying not to get involved in any altercation with his cousin. It was bad enough to see him in this disreputable state, and to see Ann so down-at-heel, without adding to the misery. He regretted, more than he could say, his earlier behaviour to Marshall when he had called him a "thief" and a "blackguard". He wanted to unsay the angry words, to smooth over troubled waters, to heal the family divisions. The healing process was proving to be difficult.

"Nonsense! They, that so-called 'government' of ours, want to know who owes them taxes. You see, Richard, you are the government agent for extorting money!"

Opening his writing-case and the ledger, Richard was going to get this business over and done with as soon as he could.

"Now. Your name first." He spoke as he wrote, *"Marshall Porter, aged 33, farmer…"*

"Don't write 'farmer'. That's what I'm saying. If you write 'farmer', they get you for more taxes. Write *'agricultural labourer'* instead, eh?"

So Richard did as he was asked, with the growing suspicion that, despite all his own sense of pride and high ideals about the importance of the day's work, Marshall might just be right.

George brought in the ale, and set it down on a small, roughly hewn oak table to the side.

"Thank you, George," Richard said, but could not resist asking, "Is your mother coming to join us?"

"No, sir."

"Don't call him 'sir'!" shouted Marshall. "He's no better than you for all his fine clothes and so-called authority. You are a gentleman's son, and don't you forget it."

With a natural gift of diplomacy, George replied to his father, "No, sir."

Richard got on with his task.

"Mrs Ann Porter, wife, aged 32, born Wilburton," he wrote.

Marshall began to laugh. "I see you remember all those details well enough."

Richard sighed, but said nothing, hoping the tension would be diffused of its own accord.

"You know, Richard. I've often thought that she was destined to be Mrs Ann Porter."

Richard thought back to when he had thought the same, and had worked so hard for all those years with that ultimate fairy-tale ending.

Marshall was continuing, "If she'd married you, she'd have been Mrs Ann Porter; and she could even have married

Stephen, for he had his eye on her, and she'd have been Mrs Ann Porter there too. Three blind mice, we were, but only one led to the slaughter.

George was pretending hard to concentrate on his book faintly illuminated by the candle on its saucer. He was wondering if the three blind mice referred to himself and his two sisters, for Richard was now asking him his age and their ages.

Richard was wondering what Marshall meant by being "led to the slaughter". Perhaps it was only the drink talking!

Then Marshall began to sing, in maudlin tones,

"Three blind mice, three blind mice,
See how they run! See how they run!
They all ran after the farmer's wife,
She cut off their tails with a carving knife;
Did you ever see such a thing in your life,
As three blind mice?"

Richard dipped his pen in the little glass bottle of ink and made the last entries in the 1851 Haddenham census, to the incongruous, drunken strains of this age-old nursery rhyme, which Mrs Vinney had sung to them so often, when they were small.

Only now, Richard understood its significance.

Chapter 6

ANN

September 10th 1861

There had been much shaking of heads down at *The Plough* when the plans for a girls' school in Haddenham had first been suggested.

Samuel Thaxter had been supping his customary pint of ale in the snuggery, after his work down at the Porter brick-kiln, and had put his point of view quite forcibly to two old cronies, Jules Newell and Vincent Popple.

"I can't see no call for eddicatin' the womenfolk. Before you know it, there'll be no talkin' to them at all, they'll be that high and mighty."

"I can't see no harm in it, Samuel," Jules' opinion was always backed up with good reason. "They'll have more sense in their heads, wi' a bit of schoolin'."

Vincent Popple had been the victim of a long life with a sour wife, inappropriately named Melody. He simply had to agree with Samuel on this matter. "But what do women want with any sense. It'll just bring more trouble and argymentation. A man will have no peace at all in his own home." The very thought of this had driven him to call over to the landlord, "Joseph, bring us another jug, if you will."

"You mark my words, Jules, we'll be wearing the aprons and they'll be in our hob-nails, marchin' all over us." Samuel had stamped his workaday boots on the floor like the militia. "Marchin', marchin', marchin'!"

"Hey, Samuel, you'd think this was a parade-ground the way you're carryin' on," Joseph Metcalfe had gently admonished this regular customer, as he refilled the mugs. "What's all the row about, anyways?"

"It's this girls' school they're a-plannin'. Can't do no one no good."

"It'll do you some good," Joseph had nodded knowingly.

"How so?" Samuel snorted.

"It's to be a red-brick building, I hear, with some twenty thousand bricks being supplied down at Porters. You'll get to make all them bricks."

And that had silenced Samuel, for he would be kept in work, he would continue to wear his "hob-nails", and his Nellie would go on wearing the apron in his household, happy to see a regular wage coming in.

It was a proud day when the school bell sounded for the first time.

The committee responsible were all assembled in the main hall to give speeches and to metaphorically pat themselves and each other on the back: for they had achieved what had appeared at first to be an impossible dream.

Haddenham was only a small village, yet through sheer energy and determination, the local education committee members had gathered together enough money to build this new school. The inscription chiselled in stone above the front door was testimony to the generosity and dedication of many interested bodies:

"The School House and Premises were Rebuilt by Voluntary Contribution and Grants made by the Council on Education, the National Society, and the Diocesan Board of Education. AD 1861."

The L-shaped building itself sported seven Gothic arched windows. Needless to say, there had been much discussion as to whether such an architectural style was suitable. One faction declared that the children would be given a "more Christian education" with God-given light shining through windows which resembled those in Holy Trinity church. Another faction believed that Gothic design had become

123

altogether desecrated by the writers of the so-called Gothic tales of horror, and that the children would be "subjected to devilish influences".

However varied and heated the opinion may have been during the preceding eighteen months, now on the 10th of September 1861, the Haddenham School for Girls and Mixed Infants was about to open. All attention was focused on the bell-tower, as the single stout bell, silhouetted against the September morning sun, rang out, summoning the scholars to school.

This ringing of the morning school bell was to become a familiar daily sound in the village. We might expect that the noise would be "altogether too distracting" for poor Catherine, who lived almost next door. It would no doubt soon become a miserable toll-bell to those reluctant young ladies who, like their male counterparts in Jaques' estimation, "creep like snail unwillingly to school".

To ten-year-old Matilda, skipping through the white school gate beside her mother and small sister, the bell's resonance was a wonderful, magical beacon of sound. She was going to school at last!

"Hurry up, Ada! The bell's ringing!" she was saying impatiently to her little sister who was to be in the infants' class, followed by an excited tugging at her mother's arm, "Oh, Mama, it's my dream. It's come true!"

This day was also a dream come true for her mother. To Ann, it was heralding a bright new future.

Ann held her head high as she sat at the pianoforte at the front of the school assembly hall, her hands poised ready to play the inaugural hymn *Now Thank We All Our God*.

Reverend Cedric Tuttle, a somewhat worldly young man of the cloth, was a potential new incumbent of Holy Trinity. With his city-slicked hair, he embraced with unbridled glee today's office of opening the new school, for it afforded him the opportunity to publicly measure up to his own personal opinion of himself. He was already making the most of this auspicious occasion, imperiously grasping both sides of the new mahogany lectern, as he stood ready to begin his opening speech.

Fifty-five girls, in identical navy blue dresses with starched white collars were seated on wooden chairs of utilitarian design: not comfortable, but lasting. The girls were seated in order of their ages: the nine bigger girls of eleven to thirteen sat on the back row, the score of nine to ten year olds were grouped together on two rows in front of them, and in front of them twenty-six girls of six to eight years were seated on two rows of smaller chairs. Ranged in rows on benches near the platform, fourteen mixed infants were seated. These four and five year old girls and boys were wide-eyed, fearful and tearful. Full of awe and apprehension, they looked up at Reverend Tuttle who now presided over them, for hadn't their parents told them what an important day this was, and how they were to behave themselves? Had they been able to read or to understand Latin, the words of the school's motto, engraved on the brass plate fixed to the front of the lectern, would not have allayed their fears, for in translation they bluntly stated: "Work equals Piety: Rest equals Impiety".

All the dignitaries and worthy bodies who had helped in their varying ways to set up this school were there on the platform. They were justifiably proud, yet part of each and every one of them was saddened that old Reverend Scott, who had worked so tirelessly for this day, had not lived to see the fruits of his labour. He had died of inflammation of the lungs on Christmas Day the preceding year.

Beside Reverend Tuttle sat Miss Maud Ground, the newly appointed Headmistress, a lady of means with a mission in life to provide education for girls. Her passion was deep-rooted, and her ultimate aim was to assist females in attaining some measure of respect and equality in a world dominated by men. She secretly had no doubt that, in her small way, she was hastening the inevitable insurrection by women.

After the preliminary address of welcome and official opening of the school, Reverend Tuttle looked down towards Ann.

"Mrs Porter, I now call upon you to start up the opening chords of our first hymn. We shall sing, with joy and thanks in our hearts, hymn number thirty-nine: *Now Thank We All Our God*." He finished with a nod for Ann to begin playing.

As the first chords were played, Reverend Tuttle raised his arms as a reminder that the pupils should now stand to sing the hymn. There was a rustling as scrubbed fingers fumbled to find the correct page in their new school hymn books.

While some children sang out with the recommended "joy and thanks", there were many who could not: for they did not know the words; indeed, they could not read the words! Had they not come to school to learn how to read? Some of the faces were transformed into such pictures of misery and dismay, that they caused considerable distress amongst the kind-hearted, well-meaning adults present. Mrs Granger, from Froize End, the wife of one of the school's local benefactors, even dabbed her eyes with a lace handkerchief, "quite overcome" she admitted later to her friends in the Haddenham ladies' circle.

The less compassionate of those in the eminent platform party experienced a form of self-satisfaction: here was the blatant evidence before them that there was indeed a need for this school, and that they were laudably responsible for bringing the advantages of education to these illiterate girls. These men and women would have done well to take heed of the school's motto: pious self-praise for their work surely could not be construed as "piety", and smugly resting on their laurels could be nothing short of "impiety"!

However, Ann was oblivious to all of this as she concentrated on her pianoforte accompaniment to the hymn. She must make no mistakes, show no lack of confidence. She was now a teacher in the school, recognised in her own right.

Ann's cause had been championed by Miss Ground, as much for her education and musical talent as for the fact that she was a woman who had broken free of the shackles of an unsatisfactory marriage, a worthy female who was trying to make a way for herself in a male-dominated world.

Mrs Ann Porter's merits had first come to the attention of Miss Ground through her friend and colleague, Miss Sharpe, the same lady who had taught music to Frances and Suzanna in the seminary which they had attended in Cambridge.

"There is only one more obstacle to be overcome, before I can set my mind at rest," Miss Ground had confided in her friend, just three months before the school was due to open. "Where to find an instructress of music in Haddenham is the problem. The ladies in Haddenham who are musically proficient would not consider working in a school, and many of the women who would like to be gainfully employed, simply have limited educational talents to offer."

"My dear Maud," Miss Sharpe had said with a twinkle in her eye, seemingly ignoring the troubled expression on her friend's face, "I can see no problem there!"

"I assure you, Philippa, it is quite a dilemma, and one which is keeping me awake at night," she had retorted.

Miss Sharpe's rings and bracelets jangled as, with an arching sweep of her hand, she had brushed aside her friend's troubles. "Pooh-pooh! No need to fret. I have the very answer." She sat back in her chintz armchair in her apartment in Cambridge with a satisfied smile on her rouged lips, and Blanche, her white French poodle, on her capacious lap.

"Well, I'm all ears," Miss Ground then had earnestly sat forward, with optimistic anticipation of good news.

"Mrs Ann Porter."

"And who exactly is Mrs Ann Porter? She has never come to my notice."

"I met her in Haddenham, when I was visiting Frances Porter. You remember Frances Beales, as she was, the former pupil of mine, with whom I have kept in touch over the years?" Miss Sharpe had added as a helpful reminder.

"The one who married a brewer and had four sons?"

"They did have four sons. It was such a tragedy, you know. Four years ago, they lost their two youngest sons, little Charles and Edwin: died of croup within two weeks of each other."

"How very sad. I'm so sorry." Miss Maud Ground, for all her stalwart views, was a kindly soul, who could empathise with individuals.

"Of course, I went to pay my respects a few weeks later and to see if I could do anything to help. And that was when I met Ann Porter. She was engaged in playing the pianoforte for Frances on a daily basis, in a bid to cheer the poor woman."

"Ah, now we come to the crux of the matter! Tell me more!" Maud had been interested.

"Ann is an educated lady in her mid-forties, the daughter of a gentleman and farmer. She lives in Haddenham with her two youngest children. She is indeed a most talented musician, and what's more she has a keen knowledge of English Literature and History. That would be useful too in your school."

Miss Ground had put her hand up to stop the flow of praise for this Mrs Ann Porter. There was disappointment in her voice, "But, I'm telling you, my dear, these are the very ladies who do not require employment, and would certainly not take kindly to it even being suggested to them."

"Listen, Maud. She is a recently divorced lady," Miss Sharpe had baldly and deliberately added. She had sat back and waited for the expected reaction from her friend.

Now, most women of the day would have immediately rejected the notion of a divorcee working in a school, but Maud Ground's passion for promoting women's rights had led her to say, "She sounds like she needs our help. Philippa, you must arrange an introduction."

128

"What do we mean by the word 'history'?" Ann asked her morning class of older girls.

Not only was Ann the school's music teacher, responsible for choral work, school concerts and instruction in the playing of recorders, she was also employed to teach History and English Literature to the class of nine older girls, and neat handwriting skills to the girls in the school who could already write, and sewing to all girls over the age of eight. Hers was an ideal timetable, interesting and varied, which gave her ample opportunity to be useful, to earn some money and to be independent.

"Learning dates of kings and queens," Jessica Pyke had shouted out loudly, followed by a snigger. Jessica had not wanted to come to school. At thirteen she was very content with her lot of being a washerwoman like her mother, and like her grandmother before her.

Ann had not wanted to chastise any of the girls on this first day, but instinctively she knew that any show of wayward behaviour had to be checked at the outset, so she firmly said, "In future, put up your hand if you want to answer my questions, and then I will ask you for your answer. Is that understood, Jessica?"

Jessica thought briefly about defying this teacher, who was only the mother of her old playmate, Priscilla, but she thought better of it and said, "Yes."

"Yes, what?" Ann was going to pursue this to the last.

"Yes, ma'am," Jessica said, with growing respect.

"Thank you, Jessica." Ann smiled encouragingly at the girl, in the knowledge that there would be no more trouble from that quarter, and that the remainder of the class would have learned a simple yet vital lesson from this short episode.

She continued, "Now, if we read the word 'history', or if we say the word really slowly, we notice that it contains another word, and that other word is 'story'. That tells us a lot about what history is all about. It is a story. It is the story of what happened in the past.

"Jessica is right that there are many dates, but the kings and queens did live sometime, just as you are living today. Sometime in the future, when you are very old, your grandchildren may ask when you were born. You will tell them the date. Jessica, what year were you born?"

"Please, ma'am, 1848." She had learned her lesson.

"That's an important date in your life, and it will be important to tell your grandchildren. They may want you to tell them what happened on your first day of school. And you will tell them the story of today, the 10th September, 1861. It will be history to them."

Ann felt good inside. The girls were interested in what she had to say; their minds were being broadened. Here was a concept being put in simple terms: an understanding of each and everyone's place in history; that people today are the subjects of history books in the future; that history is the recording of real lives.

Yes, some lives are perceived as more important: Queen Victoria and her ill-fated prince consort, Albert; Isambard Kingdom Brunel and other great engineers; David Livingstone, explorer of the "dark continent" of Africa; Socrates and other Greek philosophers; Charles Darwin, whose controversial theories were turning religious precepts on their head; literary giants such as Shakespeare, Wordsworth and the poet laureate Alfred Lord Tennyson; Lord Shaftsbury and Benjamin Disraeli in the political arena; Joseph Lister and W.T. Morton in the pursuit of modern medical techniques; Julius Caesar, Lysander, Cleopatra Queen of the Nile, Queen Etheldreda, Napoleon Bonaparte and Oliver Cromwell. These were some of the famous people whose stories Ann was looking forward to telling.

But first and foremost she understood that everyone has his or her own part to play in the history of mankind, no matter how big or small. Ann believed in the rights and importance of each individual.

No wonder Miss Ground had found her so suitable!

Near the end of the afternoon, Ann's class of nine and ten year olds, Matilda being one of them, had learnt to sing *Come Lassies and Lads*. Many of them knew the tune, but few knew the words. Just before the end-of-school bell sounded, their little soprano voices rang out, in a rendering of the whole of the first verse:

"Come lassies and lads
Take leave of your dads
And away to the maypole fly.
For every girl has a sweetheart there
And a fiddler standing by."

What began as fun, when learning the next lines about who was being paired off with whom, degenerated into quarrelsomeness among three of the girls. There were two Joans in the class and one Jane; both Joans had their eye on Jimmy Banks, and Jane had a crush on his brother Johnny. Both boys attended the Arkenstall School for Boys, situated just fifty yards further down Main Street. In the words of the song, was it Johnny who went with Joan, and Jimmy who went with Jane? Or was it Johnny who went with Jane and Jimmy who went with Joan? And if so, which Joan would Johnny choose?

The sweetness of the children's voices united in song, masked an altogether darker jockeying for position, a grasping competitiveness, even at this early age, perhaps a vindication of William Blake's *Songs of Innocence and Experience*, the volume of poems which had received much criticism at the time of their publication at the end of the previous century.

More poignantly, it reminded Ann of her own lost innocence, in the face of life's harsh experience.

Where did it all go wrong?

Her marriage with Marshall had started so well: he was a fun-loving, popular and handsome man. In 1841, theirs was a honeyed and moneyed future, with a delightful cottage as their first home. Although she had liked Marshall's cousin

Richard, and would have married him had he asked her, she believed at the time that her father had made the right choice for her in Marshall. Eighteen months later their first child had been born.

Was it when George was born?

Marshall had his son and heir, every man's requirement, but he was somehow dissatisfied with the puny infant.

"Look at his long fingers, master," Millie had enthused to Marshall over the newly-born. They had a servant in those days. Millie was sixteen and longing to have a child of her own to tend to.

"Piano-playing hands," he had said, "not farmer's. I doubt if he'll be fit to do a day's hard work." This was rich coming from Marshall who had slipped so easily into a life of minimal effort on the work front!

Was it because of Knight?

Knight had grown to be so successful, always at his father's side, making decisions, whilst Marshall the eldest was sidelined? Yet, when Marshall got home in the evenings after a long session in *The Plough*, he would always smirk and say with a slurred voice,

"It'll do him no good! The farm's mine, and there's nothing he can do about that! So he may run the whole damned shebang, all the good it's going to do him."

William had never shared with anyone, not even his family, his intentions to split his property equally between his wife, Catherine, his five sons and three daughters. Marshall's delusion of future wealth was perpetrated and perpetuated by William's silence on this matter.

Was it the drunkenness?

Over the years, drink had become an "equivocator". How true were the words of the Porter in *Macbeth*: drink "provokes the desire, but takes away the performance". The irony of these words being spoken by a Porter was not lost on Ann, as she thought of these things. At first, in their early years together, Ann and Marshall, two loving and attractive people, had enjoyed the physical side of their married life. However, what had once been pleasurable and energetic sexual intercourse, soon became a tiresome affair, with Marshall drunkenly demanding his conjugal rights and Ann responding with limp passivity.

"Just like a lettuce!" he shouted at her one night after a disastrous episode of these "conjugal rights". It was just a few months after the birth of Matilda.

"Shh. Don't shout. You'll wake the baby! George and Priscilla will hear you."

"I don't care if the whole blasted neighbourhood hears me. They should know what a life I lead." With heavy sarcasm he furthered the attack, "The loving arms of my loving wife await me every night!"

Ann had lain beside him, immobile, caught in a trap, wishing that she could have some peace, wondering if there could ever be any escape. She was slipping into an abyss of despondency, an unhappy wretch, dependent on a man who was hell-bent on self-destruction, a man who had no desire to work and provide adequately for his wife and family.

Was it their lack of money?

With relentless worsening of their financial position, Ann had contemplated seeking help from her rich father-in-law. She had broached the subject with Marshall, one morning when he was in reasonable temper.

"You will do no such thing!" Marshall was adamant.

"Have you no consideration even for your son?" she had demanded.

She had thought Marshall momentarily hesitated, perhaps considering the future for their delicate son. Marshall had been right there: with fine bones and a quiet nature, George was certainly not made of farming stock.

She had continued to press home what she perceived as an advantage, "He needs an education, befitting a gentleman's son. Your father would surely help pay for that!"

But Marshall had held fast to his resolve. He would never go cap-in-hand to that father of his.

Was it the rumours?

She knew her husband to be an attractive and charismatic man. In the early days she had been proud to have landed the best catch of the village. She had suspected that he found other women attractive, that he perhaps paid them undue attention. She had even heard rumours that he was being unfaithful. But one day, when Matilda was four months old, she had parked the perambulator outside Mr Rose's store, leaving Priscilla with strict instructions to carefully watch over it, while she went in to make some essential grocery purchases. She had entered unnoticed.

The store had been recently modernised, with a cash railway installed. The two shop assistants were ensconced in the oak-panelled cash office positioned at the top of a short flight of six stone steps, making themselves familiar with this new mechanism for transporting money from one end of the shop to another. They were pulling levers and giggling as metallic canisters were propelled, on overhead cables, to the haberdashery and millinery station in the middle section of the shop, to the station situated at hardware, adjoining the store-yard at the back of the shop, and to the grocery station near the front window, where Ann had stood waiting to be served.

"They put me in mind of you know what!" Holding one of the said canisters, Jenny Tanner had doubled up with laughter. This was the same Jenny Tanner who was the subject of the gossip, which Richard had overheard in *The Plough*: the girl who had been seen with Marshall down at Setchell's mill.

"Well, you should know," her friend knew the intimate details. "You have had many of your steamy times with Marshall."

"I'm not denyin' they're 'steamy' times," Jenny relished the memory of their many encounters down at Setchell's mill and lately in her own scullery, when she knew no one would disturb them. "He's my beau. We go a-courtin'.."

Ann had heard enough. She left the shop in a hurry, not wishing to make her presence known. Her mind was racing. How could Marshall treat her with such contempt? How these girls must laugh at her behind her back! How was she to hold her head up high?

She had known not where to turn.

Then Richard had appeared on her doorstep the following day, the day of the census. Looking back on that time, she knew that his visit on that April evening had been the turning point. She recalled their brief conversation: "But how are you?" Richard had said. "Are you well?" And she had replied, "You can see." She had disappeared into the children's sleeping quarters at the back of the cottage, wanting to hide in shame. She remembered placing baby Matilda back at her breast to suckle and she had sat rocking to and fro in the nursing chair long after Matilda had dropped off to sleep and long after Richard had left.

"So this is my lot," she had grimly acknowledged, tears freely flowing down her cheeks.

But deep inside her, a faint voice could be heard. It was her own voice, her teenage voice, "What would be the value of knowing in advance what each day was to bring. One would never strive for anything. There could be nothing but futile longing, and yearning for the unattainable. There would be no ambition, no long-term plans for the future." Those had been her very words at the Hospital Sunday fair, and she had said them with such sincerity and conviction.

Here she was at the end of her first day in the new school, accompanying the girls as they sang the last bars of *Come Lassies and Lads*: with an ambition realised, and a plan for the future. It had taken her ten years to achieve her present situation in life and much had happened in the process. No more futile longing now, nor acceptance of fate or blind belief in an assured future. She had done something to change her life; she had succeeded in bettering her lot; she had regained her self-respect.

Ann walked out through the white school gate with Matilda, whose outward ebullience quite matched her mother's inner excitement. Matilda was fairly bubbling over with stories of her day.

During morning assembly her friend Anna Roberts had accidentally fallen off her chair, and the two of them had stuffed their hands in their mouths, they were "laughing fit to burst". Their reading lesson with Miss Gooch was a trial, for the lady in question had peered over her pince-nez and accused Matilda of "reading too well", and demanded to know who had taught her, and how "Grouchy Goochy grew quite red in the face" when she realised that her colleague Mrs Porter was the rogue. Miss Ground's good behaviour lecture to them later in the morning had terrified the life out of them, as she had "such a severe face and such a loud voice". In the history lesson she had heard some "really interesting things about King William IV, and did you know when you call me a 'silly-billy', well that's where the name comes from, because he was a very silly king?". The sums and handwriting sessions were "good" and the singing lesson was "better still".

Ann listened to the unabated enthusiasm of this third child of hers. Schooling would open up wonderful horizons for Matilda, who had proved herself to be a capable and keen student at home.

Ann had tried to find time to give lessons to each of her children. It had not been easy, but it had paid dividends in the end. It had given each of them a solid basis for future education: George had attended Stourbridge School in Cambridge first as a pupil, and now, at twenty, he had become the youngest teacher ever to be appointed there; Priscilla, following in Suzanna's and Frances's footsteps, was currently a student at Miss Michael's Seminary for

Young Ladies in Cambridge; and now Matilda would shine at Haddenham Girls' School, until she was fourteen, when she too would go to study under the care and guidance of Miss Michael. Little Ada at almost five would not benefit from her mother's home tuition, but Ann, a realist, had no doubt that the child would fare better at school.

Ada had been collected at lunch-time from the infants' school by Rebecca Powers. Rebecca had found herself in need of a new position when she was nineteen. She had of course been nursemaid for Mrs Frances Porter's children, but, after the death of the two youngest – poor little mites – in 1857, her services had been no longer required. The Porters had sold their grand house on Main Street and had moved to *Waddington Terrace* in St Mary's Street, Ely, all within the space of a few months.

"Of course, I don't blame them," Rebecca had told Sam Powers, the journeyman who was her father, when Richard had informed her of the intended move. "There's too many memories for them in that big house. But I doubt if the mistress will ever get over it. Friends and the like come to keep her company, you know, to get her out of herself, but it's not doing much good, if you ask me. There's that music lady, a relation of hers, she comes to play the piano, and that cheers her a little, but when she's gone, the mistress is pretty low again."

"What about you, Rebecca? What will you do now?" her father had been genuinely worried, for with an invalid wife and three other mouths to feed, Rebecca was an equal contributor of the family's income.

"No worries, Father," she assured him. "I have a new position with Mrs Ann Porter, you know the lady that gives music lessons to the gentry and such like."

"How did that come about?"

"I don't rightly know, but it was offered me on a plate, so I couldn't refuse. Indeed, I didn't want to refuse neither."

What Rebecca was never to know was that Richard had secured the employment for her and paid for it. Despite his own misery in this time of acute mourning for the loss of his two little sons, he felt a responsibility for Rebecca who had served the family well over the years. Indeed, had the two boys lived, she would have remained in his employ as their nursery maid for the next five years, for she was as competent and motherly as Jessie had been to him and to his siblings when they were growing up in *Vine House*. He also had felt a deep gratitude for the compassion and affection which Ann had shown to Frances over the difficult, sad months. And he had wanted to help Ann. By suggesting that Rebecca work for Ann as a nursemaid for Ada, he was able to fulfil his responsibilities towards Rebecca, to show his gratitude to Ann, and to salve his conscience at one fell swoop!

Rebecca and Ada were waving from the window of the front room, as Ann and Matilda made their way homewards along the street, for they had been waiting there purposefully to catch the first glimpse of them rounding the corner from Main Street into Linden End.

"Mama! Mama! Mama!" Ada could hardly contain her excitement. She had had her very first day at school too, and wanted to share it all with her mother. "I played with blocks, and we did drawing on a slate and the lady made us put up our hands, like this, if we wanted to speak and…"

Ada prattled on like this for a full two minutes, until Ann said, "Enough for the moment, my dear. I must go and attend your grandfather. Has my father had a better day today, Rebecca?"

"I think so, ma'am. The house was that quiet that I couldn't help hearing every sound, you know, and his wheezing sometimes sounded bad. But I took him for a walk as far as *The Cherry Tree* and back. He managed that all right: it seemed to bring colour to his cheeks and he wasn't too short of breath neither. He's an amazin' eighty year old, if you ask me."

Richard Bailey had "retired from business" five years earlier. Well, those were his words for what had actually happened. The demand for horses slowly but surely was on the wane, and with neither of his sons-in-law willing or able to take over the running of the studfarm for him, he had been forced to sell up. The parish of Wilburton had long been in search of land close to the church to be consecrated as a new cemetery, and a deal was struck, which was satisfactory for both parties.

Knowing, as he did, about the financial problems which his daughter Ann silently endured, Richard Bailey had been so touched by her offer to look after him and house him in his old age, that he had agreed, but on one condition: that he pay her an annuity. He would take no refusal. Mr Josiah Brand, the solicitor with whom Richard Bailey had carried out his business for years, had quickly drawn up the necessary legal documents, and within two months the settlement had been concluded, an annexe had been built on to Ann and Marshall's home and Richard Bailey had moved in, along with Ann's piano which had lain dormant for years in the farmhouse.

Ann went in to her father, who was lightly dozing by the fire in the back parlour, a tartan rug over his knees. She looked fondly at this ancient man, stroked his blue-veined hands, which were folded across his chest.

"Father," she said, as he came awake, "I hear you had a long walk today!"

"A walk? No, I haven't stepped outside these four walls for many a day!"

Ann inwardly sighed, for her father's short-term memory was becoming less and less reliable, but she smiled and said, "Then we shall have to organise a walk for tomorrow. You'd like that, wouldn't you?"

"I remember my father and I would walk right over to Linden End catching eels. Oh, they were that slippery too! Maybe ten or twenty we would catch, and take them home to my mother. There's nothing like the smell of eels frying. Always made my mouth water, more than anything else!" He sat back, drifting into seventy-year-old memories.

"I'll bring you some tea and a muffin," Ann said kindly. Not long ago, her father would have wanted to know all about her day. Only last year, he would have asked her about her music lessons to the daughters of gentlemen in the parishes of Haddenham and Wilburton, and whether or not Bessie had behaved herself. Bessie was the pony which Richard Bailey had brought with him, along with the trap, expressly for Ann to use in her new line of work, to help her go further afield as a music tutor.

In the kitchen, the kettle was singing on its trivet over the fire. Rebecca was listening to Matilda's stories of the day and Ada was petting her two ginger kittens in a box beside the stove.

"He was askin' about your husband today, over and over," Rebecca said, a troubled expression on her face. "Askin' where he was, and what he was doing. I tried to tell him he wasn't your husband no more, but he couldn't take it in. He kept askin' and askin'."

"Don't worry yourself, Rebecca," Ann tried to comfort the girl, "he's not himself. He forgets things. We can't do anything about it. It's anno domini."

"It's what?"

"Old age. It's overtaken him, that's all. He's happy though, so that's the main thing."

Ann left the kitchen with tea and a muffin on a tray. She did not want to continue the conversation about Marshall, not in front of the children, especially since Matilda had no memories of him living with them and he had left even before Ada was born.

"If you think I am staying in my own house with your father, you must be stark-raving mad." Marshall had shaken his head in contempt, as Ann had announced her intention to look after her father.

"He has nowhere else to go, no one to care for him."

"Mrs Burgess can do the job!" Marshall had played this card in triumph. His father-in-law's housekeeper would do well enough.

"Mrs Burgess is old and going to spend her last years with her daughter over in Littleport."

Ann's ace had won the day. There was nothing Marshall could do or say that would change her mind.

For Marshall it had been the last straw. His marriage was a disaster! It had been degenerating ever since he had noticed his wife's frosty looks shortly after Matilda had been born. Then, over the next five years, his "conjugal rights" had been reduced to one night of sex of such a violent nature that even Marshall had been appalled the next day by his own actions. There had been the ever-welcoming arms of Jenny Tanner who loved him. But worse than all of this had been his wife working for a living. He hated her going out to give music lessons: it was a slur on his character; an advertisement that he was inadequate; and that he had failed his family. Ann had been very determined and had ranted and raved at him about "ambition" and "plans for the future" and "futile longing", sounding like words which had been rehearsed in her mind, over and over again.

Richard Bailey had moved in. Divorce proceedings had soon followed, and, although they dragged on for years, the settlement had finally come through in the late spring of this year, and Marshall had moved out.

As Ann snuggled under her feather quilt that night, she was justly proud of her secure position in the community, as an accomplished teacher in the new school, and as a lady whose worth was respected.

Yet she acknowledged that her success was not only the result of her own endeavours, and, in her prayers, she thanked with all her heart those whom she honestly believed had given freely and kindly of their help, and asked God to be good to them.

Her compassion and her determination had been her two guiding stars. They had served her well.

Chapter 7

MATILDA

Midsummer's Day 1875

Matilda, at twenty-four, was beautiful.

Sir Joshua Reynolds, the first president of the Royal Academy, would have found Matilda to be as exquisite a subject to immortalise as Mrs Siddons had been for his painting, *The Tragic Muse*. He would have represented on canvas the richness of her auburn hair contrasting with the light, iridescent blue of her eyes, for such vividness was the hallmark of his colourful portraits.

Equally, Thomas Gainsborough, one of the foundation members of the Royal Academy, would have been inspired. His own portrait of Mrs Siddons is known worldwide for its informality, as it challenged the theatricality of this well-beloved actress. He could have done justice to Matilda's natural serenity, modesty and easy grace.

As Matilda closed the door of the cottage which had been her home since the day she was born, even the most skilled artist would have found it well-nigh impossible to reflect the sadness mixed with stoicism which both clouded and enhanced her beauty. Here she was, the morning of this Midsummer's Day, saying goodbye.

She had neatly folded her few articles of clothing and some linen, and packed them into a trunk. This was a rather battered affair made of a cane structure covered in green canvas, secured with an old leather strap with brass studs. John Stokes, commissioned for the day, had carefully positioned it on the back of the landau, which belonged to her maiden aunts, Mary and Rachel. Her mother's black and white striped hatbox, containing Ann's old favourite lavender velvet bonnet, was placed inside the cab. So too were four individual bunches of pink Albertine blooms, snipped from the old climbing rose round the front door.

In her right hand, Matilda carried a lady's travel bag. It was a small carpetbag in design, a twenty-first birthday present from her mother, especially handcrafted by her in fine tapestry work. This bag contained Matilda's special family mementoes. One of these was her mother's purse, made of soft black leather, with light tan concertina compartments inside, and a small silver clasp on the outside. This purse had been a cherished possession, and well used.

"I should like you to have this dear little purse when I die," her mother, with a finely crocheted shawl around her shoulders, had said to her from her sickbed. "My father, God rest his soul, gave it to me on my twenty-third birthday. He said, 'This is a special birthday present,' and then he said. 'It's special for two reasons. First, because inside the purse you'll see a pocket, and I have bought you one of the new postage stamps that are really beginning to take off.' And inside, right enough, there was a Penny Black, made that year. That was in 1840. Such a long time ago! 'Mark my words, in a hundred years that'll be worth a fortune,' he said, 'so you pass it on to your grandchildren and they'll have a real heirloom!'"

"An heirloom, just fancy that!" Matilda had said. Knowing that stamp collecting was becoming really popular, and that a new word, "philately", had even been coined by some French enthusiast, she imagined that it might just be possible. "Wouldn't that be something nice to pass on?"

"Maybe your grandfather will be proved right," her mother had said, her eyes focusing now on a future in another century, "I half think he will."

"What was the second reason?" Matilda had asked, trying to keep her mother from drifting away into what were increasingly frequent bouts of unconsciousness.

144

"Oh, it was a strange reason really, as it turned out. He said, 'This is the last birthday you'll have as Miss Ann Bailey, for next year you'll be Mrs Ann Porter.'"

Matilda had seen the nostalgic look creep on to her mother's pale face: a look which told tales of youthful optimism mingled with dashed hopes; a look which told tales of affection mingled with disenchantment.

The Penny Black was still in the stamp compartment, a little dog-eared, and all of Matilda's commercial training led her to the realisation that the stamp's full potential value was already considerably diminished. There was no heirloom after all. All she had was a credit note made out to her for £30, her share from the sale of the cottage; this was in the purse too, in a compartment with a flap and a press-stud to keep the contents safe. In another section, Matilda had placed a neatly-folded page of jokes written by her sister Ada.

Dear Ada, how she made everyone laugh! She had spent hours gathering together jokes and trifles, amusing her play-mates at Haddenham School for Girls, and later her friends at Sutton Grammar School.

"I sometimes think you have not a serious thought in that head of yours," their mother would say to her.

For all her laughter, Ada had real enough fears, all concerning man's mortality. The jokes served as a smoke-screen. Her favourites were:

What is that which was never seen, felt nor heard and yet has a name? Nothing!

Why should we not blame the cab-men for cheating us? Because we call them to take us in!

Why are sluggards' beds too short for them? Because they are too long for them!

Why is a railway train like a vision in the night? Because it goes over the sleepers!

What is everyone doing at the same time? Growing older!

Also in the bag was Matilda's own personal miniature book, a gift from her mother just before she had become ill with tuberculosis. This little book with its purple cloth cover was also a birthday book, an autograph book, a diary and a Scripture text book all rolled into one, with an explanatory preface written by J. C. Ryle, the Vicar of Stradbroke. His introductory words were, *This little volume now in the reader's hand, is one which I have much pleasure recommending. It deserves the attention of all true Christians. A text and a few lines of a hymn for every day of the year – with a blank space opposite for recording any thought or fact that one wants not to lose – form the simple contents of this little pocket companion. Yet, simple as these contents seem, they are precisely what many a Christian wants in the midst of a bustling, hurrying, distracting world.*

Matilda had made only four entries in her little book.

In the space for December 1st, her own name *Matilda Ann Porter* had been written. Even though she had been baptised at twenty-one as Maude Louisa Matilda, her preferred name was still Matilda Ann! It had seemed somewhat bizarre to the good people of Holy Trinity, who had been in the congregation at the time of her baptism, that she should be christened with a new name and then discard it afterwards. December 1st was her real date of birth. Opposite this entry was a seemingly apt verse:

Ah! Whither could we flee for aid,
When tempted, desolate, dismay'd?
Or how each mighty foe defeat,
Had suffering saints no mercy seat?

The second entry on July 10th had been written in memory of her younger sister, *Ada Porter, died 74, buried on 13.* This fun-loving and popular girl had been suddenly struck down at the age of seventeen with influenza a year earlier, in that blistering summer of 1874, and had never recovered. Her desire to be baptised at twelve, just after her grandfather's death, had been more due to her fear that she might die young and be buried in unconsecrated ground, rather than to a strong belief in God. Indeed she had tended towards the modern idea that there may not even be a God. The feelings in the verse opposite her name were as confused as were her own:

God calling yet! – loud at my door is knocking;
And I, my heart, my ear still firmer locking:
He still is ready, willing to receive me,
Is waiting now, but ah! – He soon may leave me.

The third entry on August 6th had commemorated her older sister's marriage to John Burdett Sellers, *P.M. Porter. Married 74.* Priscilla had met John while she was working in Cambridge. He was a man with money: a Preston skip manufacturer, employing twelve men. He had come down from Lancashire mixing business with pleasure, and had met Priscilla quite by chance at the wedding of mutual friends. A man of quick and sometimes rash decisions, John had married Priscilla in the temporary church at Haddenham, and whisked her up north to a new life as mistress of *Oundle Villa*, her new home in Ashton, a suburb of Preston. Her sister Ada was barely cold in the grave!

The fourth and most recent entry had been made just six months later, on February 10th, *Ann Porter, died 75, buried on 14.* The verse for Matilda's dear mother could have been written especially for her,

'Tis not for man to trifle! Life is brief,
And sin is here.
Our age is but the falling of a leaf –
A dropping tear.
We have no time to sport away the hours;
All must be earnest in a world like ours.

Mr Brand, the solicitor who had acted on her behalf, met Matilda as she came down the stone steps of the cottage. She handed him the front door key.

"It's a sad day for you, Miss Porter," he said with real compassion for this young woman. "It's never easy moving out."

"No, indeed. Here is the key." She handed him the key to the cottage. He was due to give the same to Mr Prentice, the new owner, that very afternoon. "As they say though, one door closes and another one opens!"

Mr Brand nodded. This young woman certainly demonstrated considerable composure, particularly after all that she had been through.

"Does that sound harsh to you?" she suddenly asked.

"Not harsh," he responded honestly. "I would say sensible."

"My mother always used to say, 'There are so many opportunities for you in this world. They are there, waiting for you. All you have to do is to go out there and find them.'"

"That sounds like good advice," this ageing man said. His legacy work over the years had meant listening to many bereaved people quoting verbatim what the deceased loved ones had said before they departed this world. He was thinking that, had he kept a record of all the pieces of advice he had heard, he would have been able to publish a book of maxims equalling those of the very best of the philosophers. Inwardly toying with irreverent wordplay, he invented a name for such a book: *Brand New Maxims*!

Matilda continued, "She made me promise something."

This would be another piece of advice to put in his book. "What was that?" he asked.

"'You must promise me that you will never sit back longing and yearning.' So you see, I am at the start of my quest for a new life."

"I wish you luck, Miss Porter," he said with sincerity. "Your mother was a fine woman. With her words as your guiding principles, I have no doubt that you will find what you are looking for. Health and happiness to you!" he said in parting and he raised his hat to her.

"My dear, we shall miss you so much." Rachel was sitting on the chaise longue beside her sister Mary.

"Oh yes," rejoined Mary, "so much!"

The morning light filtered asymmetrically through the frayed curtains at the front window. How their mother, Catherine, dead these eight years, would have turned in her grave to have seen time's relentless destruction on her imported Belgian lace! No doubt this would have been yet another of life's distractions to her, she who had known nothing but luxury and gifts of eight healthy children from her doting husband, William.

To strangers, her two fading daughters matched their surroundings. Now in their mid-forties Mary and Rachel – or was it Rachel and Mary? – might be taken for twins. They looked alike with their pale blue eyes, and, whereas theirs were as ever insipid, weak and watery, Matilda's pale blue eyes, in comparison, seemed to positively glow with an inner light. Modern hairstyles had passed these two ladies by: their thinning fair hair, now with threads of silver, had been parted in the middle and scraped back into identical tight buns. The coiffure of twenty years ago now did them no justice. They sat together, in mirror-image poses with their hands folded neatly in their laps, a lace handkerchief at the end of their sleeve in readiness for the fond farewells, and their heads cocked ever so slightly to one side: Rachel's to the left and Mary's to the right. They were still wearing mourning garb for their dead father, a stark reminder that he was the reason for their present state.

To Matilda, they were her maiden aunts. Matilda knew nothing of their kindness to Frances when she had been in need of people to cheer her. They had, however, in their own quiet way been kind to Matilda herself over the past eighteen months. In the old days, their little acts of kindness had blossomed from a half-hearted altruism, "visiting poor dear Frances, as it helped to pass the time": but their kindness to Matilda had been something different, a kindred feeling, for they too had known suffering and sadness. Unlike Matilda, they had been totally unprepared and unschooled in how to deal with life's buffets and a relatively impecunious existence, so, in the face of their own troubles, their freely-given compassionate generosity to Matilda, in her time of need, was the product of true Christian charity. It was they who had suggested that John should take Matilda to the station. It was the least they could do!

"But we will write, will we not?" asked Matilda. She was an excellent epistolarian, and hoped that Mary and Rachel would be added to her list of regular correspondents. Though somehow she doubted if they would have much to say, as theirs was a dull life, made duller now by their so-called poverty. What had once been a wonderful round of parties, after their sister Edna had married her Mr Jones, when they were eligible maidens waiting to be espoused, had become a series of "at-homes", but now that they were no longer rich, even these afternoon invitations were becoming a rarity.

"Oh yes, we will write... pages and pages and pages!" promised Mary.

"And you will write to tell us how you get on?" Rachel added.

"I am sure you are doing the right thing, you know." Mary suddenly looked serious, pursing her lips, and nodding her head to affirm the rightness of the decision.

Mary and Rachel had, in their own way, been instrumental in securing a foothold for Matilda in her new life. It was they who had written to Frances, in one of their monthly letters, and told of the problems facing their young niece.

"There is no one to help her," they had written in their joint communication, "and we have absolutely nothing to offer, you know."

Frances had responded post haste, for hadn't Matilda's mother helped her in her time of mourning for her two dead sons. Such a long time ago, but Frances never forgot a good deed. It was her fervent belief that it was her duty to help

Ann's daughter. She had communicated by penny post the very sentiment to her two Haddenham friends.

"Of course, I shall do everything I can to help," she had written. "Only the other day, my dear Richard and I were considering the advantages of securing the services of a lady's companion, for I tend to get so down in the dumps these days now that Alfred and Frank have moved away. Did I tell you how well they are both doing? Their father is so proud that they have continued in brewing, but I find it quite incomprehensible why they had to move away from home to do it. I miss them so much. And he needs someone to help with bookkeeping and all those nasty things to do with business.

"I understand that Ann's daughter is quite a marvel with figures. Perhaps I can mention to my dear Richard that she is desirous of a situation. What do you think? Please reply by return.

"Yours ever, your affectionate and grateful friend, Frances."

As Matilda said her goodbyes, she was so touched by her aunts' tears that she said, "It is not really goodbye, you know. As the French say, it is only *au revoir*." Inwardly she thought it probably was goodbye. She certainly had no plans to come back to Haddenham, and she would not be in a position to invite her aunts to visit, for she would have no place to call her own.

Her aunts stood together on the doorstep, waving their damp handkerchiefs, a pitiable duo with little to look forward to in life and fewer expectations. This was Matilda's last view of them, as the landau pulled away. She thought how ill-equipped they were to manage their own affairs and how difficult it must be for them to live on a fraction of the money they had been used to. What had her grandfather, William, been thinking of?

William's actions had been in accordance with his lifelong views. We may remember how he had deeply felt the injustice meted out by his own father in leaving all to the eldest son, and none to him, and how he had determined to make something of himself and own the best farm in the area. He had believed that everyone should be given equal shares and had made up his mind in those early days to distribute his land and property equally amongst his eight children, so they would all have the opportunity to make something of their lives, from equivalent financial springboards.

No one had known of these intentions until one fateful September day in 1870. It was during the grouse-shooting season and many sportsmen, clad in tweed jackets, plus-fours and deerstalker hats, carrying shotguns, were out and about on the land given over especially for this sport during the season. William and his bailiff had been doing a tour of inspection round his various farms, checking which fences were in good repair and which needed attention. For some unaccountable reason, Ned, his sturdy hunter, normally so reliable, reared up as a shot was fired and a grouse flew up in a flurry of feathers from behind a nearby bush. William was thrown from the horse and landed awkwardly.

He had a fractured right hip and severe internal pain. Lying in bed, after the surgeon had left, William knew with certainty that his farming days were over. He called for the services of Ezekiel Smith, a conveyancer, there and then.

In the presence of Marshall, Knight, Edna, Mary and Rachel – Henry and Jacob were unable to be contacted at such short notice, and Stephen had at last reached his promised land – Mr Smith had begun to draw up the transfer documents.

"Your father is proposing that ownership will be given to each of his eight children," and he traced down their names with his index finger as he read, "Marshall, Stephen, William Knight, Henry, Jacob, Edna, Mary and Rachel."

Imagine the scene! Marshall was flabbergasted. Never in his wildest dreams had he considered that his father would go against custom. He turned to Mr Smith.

"I suggest you put your damned writing case away, Ezekiel. My father is clearly not in sound mind."

"My body may be broken, but there is nothing wrong with my mind," William said. "Continue, Ezekiel!"

"That an equal portion of his land, eighteen acres apiece, be conveyed this day to each and every one of the aforesaid."

Marshall turned on his father. "You're a thief and a blackguard!" he shouted, the words all too familiar.

"You may call me 'blackguard' if you wish; it is all I would expect from you. But a 'thief'? How so? How can I steal something which is my own?" William clutched his side: the pain was getting worse.

Now Marshall faced Knight. "I suppose you engineered this charade! Always had your sights on more than your due, didn't you? Always thought to do me out of my birthright inheritance!"

"You never had that kind of inheritance!" William was breathing heavily. "It was never my way, and never my intention."

"It was always mine!" The shocking truth was beginning to sink in, and Marshall looked close to a show of violence, or a show of tears. It was difficult to know which way his disappointment would now manifest itself.

"Never!" William's blunt contradiction was too forceful to be challenged.

Marshall's tack therefore became one of wheedling rationale. "What good will land at Hillrow do Stephen in Florida, in heaven's name? Have you even thought of the practicalities? It's nothing short of madness! Talk to him, Ezekiel. Make him see sense."

"Your brother can sell it to the highest bidder, or get a tenant farmer in," Mr Smith was the only one who had thought this through. "My partner in Ely is a land agent experienced in this type of conveyancing. He would be of great assistance in the matter." Mr Smith could also envisage some fat fees coming their way too!

Marshall was not to be put off so easily. "I mean, think of Rachel and Mary! Eighteen acres would keep no one in any degree of comfort! What do they know about business? They couldn't afford to hire anyone to run such a paltry little farm. They'd have to sell, and live on bank interest! Have you even considered their future?"

"Your father wishes also to give the house to Mary and Rachel, on condition that he remains here for as long as he lives."

"And when he dies, they'll have a huge house to run, with too little money in the bank to do it. Idiotic, through and through!"

To Marshall's credit, despite the shattering of his own personal future, he seemed to be the only one who considered these two vulnerable women. Now they would have nothing to offer potential husbands: neither youth nor a fortune.

Knight spoke not a word: he had worked hard and bought land in his own right, and his first wife, Sophia, had come with a sizeable acreage of land out at Staple Leys where he now lived, and his second wife, Jemima, had come with money inherited from the estates of her two former deceased husbands. His father's decision would bring him extra land, which he had not bargained for, but was nevertheless most welcome.

Edna was happily married to Thomas Jones in Littleport, and they had plenty of good farming land there. They would sell the eighteen acres at Hillrow and invest in more modern farm machinery at Littleport. Her lively mind had all this worked out in a trice! She had wanted to rush back immediately to Thomas to tell him the good news. It was as well she did not: it would have been most unseemly in hindsight, as this was the last time she would see her father alive, for he died the following month.

Mary and Rachel had been bemused by it all. Their father's decision was his, and not to be questioned. They had not really understood what the animosity was all about. They knew so little about the real world. But what they did know was that "dear Marshall" – as they were to refer to him thenceforth! – was thinking about them and looking after their interests. Having held Marshall low in their estimation for so many years, they revised their opinion there and then! They now had no doubt that, had Marshall inherited all, there would have been a place for them in his house. He would have looked after them, as all unattached sisters were taken care of by the head of the family. They had said as much to Matilda on a number of wistful occasions.

As Matilda thought about this, she could not in all conscience agree with her maiden aunts. "Dear Marshall" had left her own mother, with three children still to support. Perhaps if her grandfather, William, had told the family of his intentions to split the property a long time before, then things might have been different: her father might have made something of his life; he might not have been so lazy, dissipated and later disillusioned with life. He might have been content with his family and her parents might not have divorced. Yes, she thought, her grandfather William had a lot to answer for!

Marshall had sold his eighteen acres, but, as we might have predicted, he did not use the good services of Ezekiel Smith and partner. They had done too much damage, in his opinion! He had begun to make a go of things, at last. He had set himself up as a butcher opposite Mr Rose's store, well situated to attract customers.

It was a fairly modest establishment: a conversion of the parlour and scullery of the house which had used to belong to the Tanners. Old Mr Tanner had died and Jenny had long since flown the nest, in search of employment in Earith, once she had grown tired of her "steamy" adventures with Marshall. As he sharpened his cleaver on the oiled strap kept supple for the purpose, Marshall grimly amused himself with the irony that he was now cutting up animal carcases in the same scullery which had seen many a scene of unadulterated and adulterous animal passion!

Now the butcher's shop stood empty. Marshall had disappeared without trace in 1872. He knew nothing of his son's death, or Priscilla's marriage to John Sellers, or the death of Ann or the death of his youngest daughter, Ada.

Matilda realised that he would know nothing of her either, just as she knew nothing of him. She suddenly felt very alone.

Matilda had two more visits to make before she left Haddenham for good. The first of these was to be a sad goodbye to her family, now in Wilburton.

She stepped out of the landau outside Wilburton Parish church. She was protected from the strong summer sun by the ancient yew in the centre of the graveyard, as she bent over the grave of her maternal grandfather, Richard. She read the fancy copperplate inscription on the gravestone: *In loving memory of Richard Bailey, born 1781, died May 4th 1868 and his beloved wife Ruth born 1776, died September 30th, 1823.* Matilda, with a solemnity befitting her feelings of respect for these her grandparents, laid one of the four bunches of Albertine roses across the bodies of the "dearly departed".

Then she walked across the road to the new graveyard, the tract of land bought by the parish committee from her grandfather at the time he had decided to sell off all his property.

This plot of land was still in a pristine state. Yew trees on the periphery had been planted less than fifteen years ago, and as yet had not even begun to simulate the imposing elegance of the two-hundred-year-old yew in the parent burial ground. It was a bleak spot, and in mid-winter was completely desolate and windblown. There Matilda's mother and sister were buried side by side, open to the summer sun and the winter snows. Ann had been buried in the snow.

Matilda thought back to that time. How strange it had all seemed: almost surreal!

Richard had been there. Matilda had no idea why her father's cousin should attend the funeral. Yet there he was, wearing his top hat wound round with black crepe ribbon. There had been something else though: it had been the expression on his face. Matilda would never forget it. He seemed to be mourning, but mourning for what? What had her mother meant to him? It was very confusing and unreal.

"Your mother was a wonderful woman," he had said as he stood beside her, at the grave.

Matilda had found no adequate words. Instead she said simply, "These are nature's teardrops, you know."

She had held up a small posy of six or seven early snowdrops for him to look at. He hadn't known what to say to this girl. She placed the delicate flowers on the mound of earth over her mother.

"They will dry, like all tears. And that's when the spring flowers will take their place, and we will be happy again."

She placed a bunch of summer roses on each grave, and abruptly walked away. The time for tears was over. She had shed enough.

Back in Haddenham, they stopped outside Holy Trinity.

"You've only got a few minutes, miss, if you're to catch Old Grunty," John Stokes reminded Matilda as he handed her down from the landau at Holy Trinity graveyard. "Old Grunty" was his pet name for The Grunty Fen Express, which ran twice each weekday from Sutton to Ely, calling at Haddenham on the way, and twice back from Ely to Sutton with another stop at Haddenham Halt, the station at the bottom of Main Street. Only now the street leading past *Vine House* towards Haddenham End was called Station Road. How many "Station Roads" across the country were born in those early days of the railways!

Old Henry Porter had welcomed the approaches of the advance guard officials of the Sutton and Ely Railway, and had sold off some land at Haddenham End: some four acres containing his brickyards and the brick-kilns, for the erection of a railway station; and land across Grunty Fen for the laying of tracks.

The sale of this land had been one of a number of bones of contention between Henry and Alice's "love child", Henry John, and Richard. On the one hand Richard, with his business acumen, had recognised the potential of the land down at Haddenham End for future railway development, and had persuaded his father to transfer most of it over to him beforehand.

Henry John, in retaliation, had encouraged his father to rescind his father's written intentions of leaving the brewery to Richard.

In consequence, Henry's will, dated January 1870, had been changed in Henry John's favour less than three months before Henry had died in June 1871. What had made it all the more disturbing was the fact that the old man was senile and hardly able to think clearly for more than a quarter hour at a time! Richard would not inherit the brewery after all, only the "utensils therein", and on his death, his two sons Alfred and Francis would each be given one hundred pounds in lieu.

Henry John had been left *Vine House* too. Richard had seen the writing on the wall long ago, and he had known deep down that *Vine House* was lost to him, but the reality in black and white in his father's will had been a bitter pill to swallow. The rift between the youngest and oldest brothers was one which was almost impossible to heal, and the two branches of the family grew apart. More family divisions!

Matilda stepped over the rubble, which was strewn irreverently across the consecrated ground surrounding Holy Trinity church. The builders were busy erecting a new spire. In fact, they had been busy building this spire for the past three years, for hadn't her sister, Priscilla, married in the temporary church because this one was out of commission at the time!

158

"Watch your feet, miss," one of the labourers called out.

"Mind you don't get hit on the head from falling masonry," said another.

"Can't you read the notice!" another, less civil, person called out.

Indeed there had been a disclaimer placard attached to the gate, but, as she swung it open, it meant little to her. "You enter this area at your peril!" it read. To Matilda, it seemed ironic that those who had already entered in their coffins, drawn by the one remaining Haddenham bier, were hardly likely to be further harmed by what life, or steeplejacks, could cast down upon them!

She trod carefully through the broken bricks and mortar, noting the slates and stones stacked neatly in readiness for the next stage of the construction process. She looked up at the church tower. The original spire had been deemed unsafe a long time ago, and had been demolished. Holy Trinity had done without its vertex for as long as people could remember. What a furore there had been over the funds which had been collected for the rebuilding of a new church spire! She shuddered as she remembered.

The scandal had even hit the newspapers! *Church Funds Disappear! Butcher Suspected of Theft! The Amazing Disappearing Act! Allegations Refuted! Unsolved Case of Theft!*

Matilda had not known what to think or where to turn. Funds had gone missing: that was true. Her father had gone missing at the same time: that was true. His little butcher's shop had been abandoned. She had supposed that it was easy to put two and two together, and her father, Marshall, did not have a good reputation in the town. But she had refused to accept that her father was a thief, and to her dying day was to remain resolute in that belief. And why had his cleaver and butcher's knives mysteriously vanished too?

159

Perhaps he had been murdered by vagabonds from Babylon for his knives, and then his body thrown into the river.

She had even entertained the gruesome idea that he had drowned in a drunken stupor in one of the outlying fens. She remembered the story of a body which had been found in Adventurer's Fen when it had first been drained. Maybe one day her father's body would be found lying in the blue delph at the bottom of a drained fen.

Perhaps he had seen the error of his ways and had become a missionary and joined David Livingstone in Central Africa.

Maybe he had some money over from the sale of his share of eighteen acres and had bought a ticket to travel to America on a steam-packet, to join his brother in Florida.

She was never to know what happened to him; the people of Haddenham did not know either. So the question, "Was he the Porter who stole the church funds?" became a regular focus of gossip long after the people in my story had passed on, and is still asked today in some fenland circles.

Matilda placed her last bunch of roses on the grave of her paternal grandparents, William and Catherine. They lay in the same sarcophagus, side by side, right beneath the belfry. Catherine, at rest, could no longer be "distracted" by the church bells, and William now had her all to himself at last. Heaven indeed!

Matilda looked all around, as the shafts of sunlight pointed their fingers on the gravestones of the Porters.

Poor Richard! In that moment her heart went out to him. For there lay Henry, his father who had died in 1871, leaving Alice a fine widow's annuity and her own property. There lay his baby brother Henry, dead now for almost fifty years, so long ago as to be almost forgotten; and there lay his two little sons with the sad little gravestone:

IN MEMORY OF THE BELOVED CHILDREN OF
RICHARD AND FRANCES PORTER.

EDWIN FREDERICK, DIED FEBRUARY 1 1857
AGED 2 YEARS 9 MONTHS
CHARLES BEALES DIED FEBRUARY 14 1857
AGED 5 YEARS.

SUFFER LITTLE CHILDREN TO COME UNTO ME AND FORBID
THEM NOT FOR SUCH IS THE KINGDOM OF HEAVEN.

Poor Richard! He had had more than his share of sadness. Yet in all his personal grief and trouble, he was able to extend a helping hand to her in her time of need! She was filled with feelings of humility, awe and gratitude.

A kind of inner peace and serenity was born in her in the graveyard on that Midsummer's Day. She held her head high and made her way across the uneven ground back to John Stokes and the waiting landau. A new life awaited her: she must not miss her train.

"If it would be no trouble to you, miss, would you give this to my brother," John Stokes said, indicating a wicker basket with a red and white checked cloth covering the contents. "It's quite light really."

Matilda was to be met by John's younger brother, Simon, who had gone with Richard to Ely as his coachman and to look after the dray horses used in the brewery.

"It's no trouble," Matilda said.

But John was continuing to persuade her, all in one breath! "You see, it's my Janet, she's such a forceful woman, I never can say no to her, I mean that's how we got married, she wouldn't take no for an answer, and she wanted to send over some of her raspberry jam to Hettie, that's my sister-in-law, our Simon's missus."

"Honestly, it's no trouble. There will be a porter there to help, you know!" Then she began to laugh. It was such a well-worn joke, one that had been played on her many times by her school-friends, when she had gone to Sutton Grammar School by train. And now the joke was on her!

"It's very good of you."

"Is there any special message for your brother?"

"Just say we look forward to seeing him and Hettie and the family at Christmas." He spoke slowly, as if Matilda were writing down the words in her head. "Oh yes, and tell him that Mother is much improved, and can move her right arm a bit now."

The Haddenham station-porter now appeared with a hand-barrow. In no time he had loaded up with Matilda's battered green trunk, her hatbox and Janet Stokes' basket, and set off at high speed through the station doors and onto the platform. By the time Matilda had caught up with the porter, John Stokes was on his way back up Station Road, past *Vine House*. He would soon be passing Holy Trinity and the crossroads with the old finger signpost; then finally be back home with his Janet.

Matilda sat on the slatted wooden seat on the platform. In bad weather most people would sit in the waiting room, but today the weather was too perfect to spend indoors, if at all possible.

The two sets of rails were gleaming in the sunshine. She remembered learning in school that the distance between the rails was four feet eight and a half inches. She had forgotten the reason, though, for that odd measurement. Was it something to do with metres and centimetres, which had been adopted in the rest of Europe? She was in no mood to start doing calculations! There would be enough of those to do soon. So the question remained unanswered.

On the other side of the railway tracks two railroad workers were leaning on their shovels. One was our friend Samuel Thaxter, who had found employment with the Ely and Sutton Railway Company, after the Porter brick-making business had been sold. He was looking across to Matilda and nodding in her direction as he spoke to his workmate, a Joseph Gateson, a young man of twenty-four who had married too young and found it hard to keep his eyes off attractive women.

"You're right there, Joseph, she is a pretty girl. And how she has come through all her troubles, I'll never know."

"You mean her mother dying?" the younger man asked, unimpressed. When his mother had died, it had been a matter of course, something expected, and nothing to make a fuss about. He had only been seven at the time!

"There's more to it than that. There was all that upset about her father. They said he stole the church funds and ran off to America with them. Lord Hardwicke had to pay for the new steeple as it turned out."

"Well, he can afford it," said Joseph, unimpressed too with the so-called generosity of the rich.

"That's not the point! You see, no one rightly knows what happened. For all we know the thief could be right here in our midst, even yet. Now there's something for you to think on."

"That Will Barleycorn has a shifty look. Maybe he's the one."

"I heard tell he got married out there too!"

"Who?" Joseph showed a spark of interest. "Will Barleycorn?"

"No! Marshall Porter. Though I tell you this: she'd need to be long-suffering. Even that Jenny Tanner got fed up with him, and that's saying something, for she liked anything in trousers."

"She sounds a bit of all right then!" Joseph unexpectedly said.

"You be careful now. What'd your Mary say, if she heard you a-speaking adulterous thoughts like that?"

"I'd be out on my ear!" Joseph laughed, to brush the whole matter aside as a joke, though secretly he thought that he could have a night or two of fun with Jenny Tanner, and it would not do any harm.

Matilda knew they were talking about her. But she held her head high, for she was leaving all this behind. All the talk, all the tittle-tattle!

Round the bend came "Old Grunty", puffing and panting, a huge monster of a locomotive. It let out a loud hiss of steam as it stopped. Carriage doors were opened and passengers poured onto the platform. Normally the train stopped at Haddenham Halt just long enough to let the passengers off and on. There was never any dillying or dallying. There was no time for prolonged farewells, just time for the luggage to be put in the luggage van and the passengers to take their seats. Matilda sat in the first-class carriage, a plushy compartment with velvet seats and comfortable headrests, antimacassars, pictures of famous British castles on the walls and a net rack up above the seats for small items like umbrellas and top hats. She had never travelled first-class before, but Richard had sent her the ticket. She supposed that if she was to be a lady's companion to Frances, and to assist Richard in his bookkeeping, then it was only fitting that she should travel like a lady.

She sat back in the luxurious seat, the whole six-seater compartment to herself, and with a shrill blast on the guard's whistle, the train slowly began to move. As the train picked up speed, she watched as the station and Haddenham and her memories were left behind, till they were no more than specks on the flat landscape of the past. She fixed her eyes on "The Ship of the Fens" on the distant horizon, and fixed her mind on her future.

As the train was drawing into Ely Station – a large complex of buildings, ticket offices, waiting rooms, numerous platforms, shunting yards, water towers, coal stocks, signal boxes, turntables and hundreds of people milling about – Matilda was drying her eyes. All of her resolve had melted as Ely Cathedral had got closer. She did not mean to get upset: it had all come upon her so unawares. She had been thinking about the history of the Cathedral, and about Queen Etheldreda.

On Friday 17th October, 1873, St Etheldreda's Day, there had been special services in the cathedral, as a farewell to Bishop Browne who was leaving the Diocese. There had been a grand luncheon in *The Lamb Hotel* and in the evening there had been special entertainments for the National School managers and teachers. George, her brother, had attended this function, and had written home to his mother enthusing about the honour of being an invited guest and his hopes for his future in education. On the anniversary of this very day, one year later, George had died, in a little place called Poplar. Another victim of tuberculosis, she was told. The memories could no longer be held at bay. First Ada, then George, then her mother!

As the train came to a halt, she was composed again. She would not give in again; she would not be taken unawares again. Of that she was certain, whatever might befall.

Simon Stokes was not unlike his older brother, but of a stocky build, a man used to manual labour. Yet his bearing showed that he was used to giving orders too. At fifty-two, he ran a good stable yard; the stable lads knew what was expected of them; the carters never had any complaints for the haulage carts were always in excellent repair and were safe on any highway; and above all, Mr Porter was satisfied with his work and paid him a handsome wage.

He was helping Matilda into the brougham. This was a new covered carriage bought in readiness for Matilda.

"Mr Porter said you was to have the use of this brougham. Any time you and Mrs Porter need to go into the town, you let me know, and I'll have it ready for you in two shakes of a cat's whisker!"

"Thank you, Mr Stokes, that's very kind."

"This is Magdalene," he said as he stroked the muzzle of the sleek black mare. Then he jumped up onto the coachman's seat. "She's a reliable horse, she is. Very obedient and strong too! Giddup there, Magdalene!" and they were off.

In the intervening years since we were last in Ely – you remember that February day in 1822 when there was mist and frost all around? – we become aware that time is really the grim reaper.

Some things have changed forever as time and progress march forward hand in hand. The old cottages over on Babylon are still there, but the cheery bargees are no more. The railway put paid to their livelihood.

Some things remain almost unchanged, but buildings fall to ruin and old crafts are in their dying throes. If we look again into the window of the basket-maker's old cottage to watch the osiers being skilfully woven into eel traps, there is Paul Gotobed making an eel grig, that large variety of eel trap found only in the Fens, but he is one of the last remaining basket-makers in the city.

The Thursday February market still is held, but Madame Zorra and her friends have no power to enthral young listeners, who have been educated and know that one's future cannot be predicted.

The Lamb Hotel, that old posthouse and coaching inn, is still there in the middle of the town, still holding its own, but for how long can it continue to be a thriving concern, with the railway taking the travellers away from the old coaching route through the town? How long can the menu, a "Lucretian feast" of tender duckling, succulent asparagus and creamy cheese of Cottenham, continue to lure the customers?

And St Mary's Street? What changes are there as we approach our destination. *The Cromwell Arms* is now a privately owned house: we can imagine William's disgust at such a turn of events. St Mary's fourteenth-century church spire still reaches up over the treetops, but round the corner, where the horse fair had once been held, the green in front of the Chantry is no more. For there stands *Waddington Terrace*, our destination. It was Matilda's destination on that Midsummer's Day of 1875.

Canon Waddington, that worthy man who had trained his singers to reach heavenly heights had succumbed after all to more worldly concerns. He had sold the land between The Chantry and St Mary's Street to the highest bidder: property developers. As it turned out, they were men of some breeding and culture whose architectural designs could not have offended even their most scathing opponents, for there had been many who believed that the new buildings in that spot would "ruin the fine aspect of the Chantry and indeed the overall beauty of St Mary's Street and its medieval church".

Matilda had known nothing of this. She had only been to Ely a few times, but as she had always gone by train, she had never had reason to walk as far down St Mary's Street as this, for it was at the other end of the town from the station, and her priority had been to visit the shops and the bustling Thursday market.

She was ushered into a spacious drawing room, with wall hangings, mirrors, large landscape paintings all around. Millicent, the young maid, had taken Matilda's travel cloak and her bonnet to the room on the first floor which was to be hers.

Then she returned, saying, "The mistress is quite poorly again today, and she sends her regrets that she cannot welcome you to your new home. Mr Porter will be down to you directly. If you would care to take a seat, ma'am."

Millicent was not quite sure how to address this new person. She knew that Matilda was a distant relation of the master's, but she also knew that she was to be employed by the master. It was all very confusing, so she would call her "ma'am" until told to do otherwise. She also thought it expedient to drop a small curtsy, as she left, just in case!

When Richard entered, Matilda immediately jumped to her feet. He had not expected this and his prepared speech of welcome was temporarily postponed.

Matilda too had not expected what she saw, for Richard now sported whiskers all round his chin, like an upturned halo, she thought. She did not know what to say.

He smiled. She smiled.

Memory plays wicked tricks! Christmas Day, chestnut curls, blue eyes and oh such a lovely smile!

He smiled again, pushing the memories back into that inner compartment once more.

"Welcome, Matilda!" he extended his hand to her. "I trust you will be happy here."

How his deep brown eyes shone with warmth and welcome! As she took his hand, her heart started to beat fast. He was such a good looking man! She knew that he must be close on sixty, but he was so athletic and lithe! Her breathing quickened in pace. What could be happening to her? He was old enough to be her father, and married!

"I am sure I will be most happy, Richard," she said, trying desperately to keep that composure she promised herself.

"Come!" he said. "Let me show you round the house!"

Chapter 8

RICHARD

May 20th 1887

"Good morning, Stokes! Fine day!" Richard addressed Jimmy Stokes with some reference to the weather every morning, and thereupon a discussion about cloud formations, temperatures, heatwaves, snowstorms, fenland mists, or rain would ensue. Today was no exception. "Do you think it will last?"

"Well, you know what they say: 'Red sky at night, shepherd's delight!' It was a ruddy sunset last night, so I predict that there will be not a cloud in the sky."

"That's good."

"What time should I have the carriage ready, sir?" Jimmy inquired, for his master had expressed a wish to be taken to the Thursday market.

"Two o'clock, Stokes. Make sure you're on time!" Richard always said this, yet Jimmy Stokes had never once been late!

Jimmy was true to his family tradition of reliability. He had followed in his father's footsteps and had become head of Mr Richard Porter's stable-yard. Simon Stokes had died quite suddenly five years before, and Jimmy had been promoted to chief ostler, in charge of the ten Suffolk punches used in Richard's new haulage firm. At thirty-eight, Jimmy was hard-working, and had re-organised the stable-yard situated behind *The Eagle* brewery, so that Mr Porter's two concerns – the brewery and his carrier business – could be operated from the same base. The brewery had been opened in 1869, set up using all the equipment from the old family brewery in Haddenham, but the new haulage business had been opened much more recently, during the cold winter of 1883.

During that particular December, when temperatures dropped well below freezing and all the surrounding fens and waterlogged fields had frozen over, independent observers had shaken their heads sadly at that juncture.

"He's an old man! What would an old man want with a new business?" Jeremy Smiley, one of the regulars in *The Eagle and Lamb* had spoken his mind, forgetting that he sat in the snug of the said "old man's" hostelry.

"What age do you reckon he is, then? He can't be all that old!" Philip Banks, his life-long friend and neighbour was prone to contradict. "He looks fit and healthy enough to me!"

"He must be in his late sixties!"

"Get away!" Philip had wanted to press his point. "Only last week I saw him skating over on the pond at Lynn Road, and doing all kinds of fancy steps! He couldn't be even sixty!"

"Well, let's see," said Jeremy, scratching his chin as he worked out the mathematics of his proof. "When he and his family first came to Ely, I remember that we all came to the conclusion that we were the same age as his missus and the difference between their ages was about eleven years, so that puts him at about eleven years older than we are. Now you and I are both going on fifty-six, so that puts him at sixty-seven, give or take a year."

"Well, he's truly amazing then. I mean he was there, keeping up with that young Albert Tebbit, you know that speed-skater, the one who's tipped to win the Duddlestone Cup one day."

Jeremy and Philip had said nothing for a while, just enjoying the warmth of the fire on that bitterly cold evening.

Then Philip continued the conversation about Richard Porter. "I can't see a carrier business doing well, not these days with the railways. I mean, if you wanted to transport goods to Cambridge, it takes a whole day to get there by the turnpike."

What these two worthies had not taken into account was the fact that Richard was transporting his ale to public houses in Cambridge, and did not want the barrels tampered with or even drained by unscrupulous railroad workers. It was safer to send them by road.

"It's his wife spurs him on," Jeremy had shaken his head. Women were always at the root of silly decisions! "Imagine having a mortgage hanging round your neck like a millstone."

"He won't have a mortgage: he'll have paid outright!"

"No, I tell you, he has. My girl, Lizzy, told me he had borrowed six hundred pounds to set up the business!" Lizzy worked for four shillings and threepence a week as a clerk for Mr Bailey, a money-lender, who arranged mortgages.

"He'll have to keep on working till he's in the grave, to pay all that off!" Philip shook his head sadly, for he was a man who had paid rent all his life and would have to go on doing so for the rest of his days: he had always envied those happy men who could afford a mortgage because one day it would be paid off. This story about Richard Porter turned Philip's view of money matters upside down.

Contrary to the expectations of all such doubting Thomases, the carrier business had flourished, and the mortgage had been paid off long ago. The railway may have been in direct competition, but many manufacturers and farmers preferred the relative security of personal attention, when it came to getting their goods to Cambridge for distribution.

As a sprightly seventy-six year old, who had never had a day's illness in his life, Richard had never entertained the idea of selling up and living the comfortable life of retirement. He employed a manager to take charge of the haulage business, and a chief brewer had been installed in *The Eagle*, but he still popped in to both premises every morning to oversee decisions. He always walked there and back, no matter what the weather was like, striding out in his frock-coat and top hat; and never without his father's brass-handled cane – for sentimental reasons.

He was just returning from these morning visits, and, satisfied that everything was running smoothly, he could now concentrate on the real business of the morning. After a few months of sensible discussion and gentle persuasion, Richard had been convinced that it would be expedient for him to make a new will. Mr Joseph Rogers, his solicitor, was to arrive at ten o'clock for that express purpose.

When Richard entered the office on this beautiful spring morning, Matilda was seated at a light oak roll-top bureau, poring over the monthly accounts. She had always liked this downstairs room in *Waddington Terrace* because it looked out onto the walled garden at the back of the house. Over the years, from this very room, she had watched the seasons come and go in this quiet, secluded garden, but spring was her favourite.

The Victoria plum tree stood proud and tall in the corner near the building which comprised coach-house, stable and hayloft, at the end of the garden. It was now in blossom on this April day. As long as the bullfinches kept away, there would be a fine fruit crop in the summer. The raspberry canes were beginning to sprout new leaves in the fruit patch near the sunny left-hand brick wall. Purple and yellow pansies and pink primulas were in bloom in the ornamental rockeries. Lupins and delphiniums were already showing signs of early flowering in the herbaceous borders.

On that first day when Richard had escorted Matilda round the house, he had shown her into this very room.

"I thought this might be a suitable office. It is light and airy, and it is a quiet spot." He had noted her eyes light up in approval.

"Thank you," she had said, smiling. Richard was pleased. In actual fact, she was smiling because she was remembering the words of her tutor Miss Pinkerton, in the Ladies Sutton School for Commerce. 'You would do well to adopt the quiet ways of friars, monks, bishops and nuns, for they work in undisturbed silence at their writings and calculations!' As Matilda looked out at the Cathedral belfry and St Mary's Church spire, both towering in holy, mute grandeur above the walls of the garden and over the near rooftops, she thought that both must be in league with Miss Pinkerton!

"How is it this morning?" Richard now asked, indicating Matilda's left wrist, which was bound with a white bandage.

"Still uncomfortable," she admitted, "but it is on the mend. It's only a light sprain."

"And the bruises?"

"Rather colourful!" she replied lightly.

Richard admired this kind of fortitude. It was ever her way, to put a brave face on things. However, he was concerned too.

"You really do need to look after yourself after a nasty fall like that."

Matilda had fallen down the steps on her way out through the front door the previous day, sprawling in what she imagined was a most unladylike manner at the feet of a surprised Mr Ingles, a neighbour who was out walking his cocker spaniel. Richard understood she had tripped over the brass sill at the threshold and had immediately sent for Joe, the odd-job man employed in *The Eagle*, to come and secure it properly, so that it was flush with the floor.

Matilda had not told him what had really happened: that she had been overcome with a sudden weakness and her legs had given way under her. She had fallen, that is true, but she had not tripped over anything.

"Perhaps you should let someone else do the accounts," he tentatively suggested.

"Indeed not!" she insisted, not wanting to give in. "I have always done the accounts."

Now this was not strictly the case and she knew it. Richard knew it too. Her determination to soldier on was now in jeopardy, as he raised his finger as a reminder that she had not always done the accounts.

"Now, Matilda!" was all he said, but it was enough to make her blush to recall that, three years after she had started working for him, she had left him in the lurch, and that he had had to manage for four years without her.

Matilda had spent the first three of those years in *Oundle Villa*, Preston, working as Priscilla and John's housekeeper to help them look after their four children.

Her sister, Priscilla, had written her a letter which was more of a cry for help than her normal, if infrequent, sisterly correspondence.

"My dear Matilda, I am quite alone and desolate, here in this alien northern county. I believe John's relations do try to be kind and do their best to keep me company, but I feel so surrounded by them. They are forever appearing in my house, uninvited, always offering me advice on how to bring up the children, and how to run an efficient house, and how to look after my husband and how to treat the servants. I am constricted and constrained.

"Dear sister, I long for your company, and I would prefer your help in running my home and family, above that of any other human being. Please come up north. Please come to my assistance as a companion, housekeeper, sister and friend, with free board and lodging for these few kindnesses to me.

"Your affectionate sister, Priscilla."

So Matilda had gone up north to help her sister, until she could stand it no longer! Three years was more than enough. She experienced the claustrophobia of *Oundle Villa*, a typically Lancastrian semi-detached Victorian town house in a Preston suburb, with the in-laws living next door. The problem lay with the connecting door between the two houses, for that led to the regular intrusions of the Sellers family in Priscilla's home.

Matilda could have tolerated this, for it was not really her problem, and she could have put up with the coarse loudness of the local tradesmen and the neighbours, with their "ee by gums", and their use of "thee" instead of you, and using dialect words, like "ginnel" instead of alley, and "starving" instead of cold, and contracting the definite pronoun "the" down to "t'" before every noun.

But what finally drove her away were the unwelcome attentions of her flirtatious brother-in-law, John Sellers, who took to lurking in dark recesses in the vestibule or in the landing, whenever he knew she was going about her house-keeping business on a dark evening. He would suddenly appear from the shadows and she would gasp with shock. He had taken these involuntary noises as an indication of her delight and desire.

One evening, when she had been carrying a pile of newly laundered linen to the hot-press on the first landing return, he had grabbed her from behind, and held her tight, his hands pressed on her bosom.

"Get off!" she whispered, so as not to attract her sister's attention, for this was altogether untoward and despicable behaviour. Naturally, John thought she was whispering because she did not want anyone to interrupt them!

"Got you now, my lovely!" he whispered in her ear, breathing heavily.

She had been unable to defend herself with all the sheets, pillow-cases and towels piled high in her arms, and he began to squeeze her breasts and then rub his hands down her body, before she had managed to get free.

She had written to Richard, that very night and sent the letter first class in the early morning post the very next day. She asked him to please help her find a new position immediately, and within ten days, Matilda had packed her bags, said goodbye to a tearful and uncomprehending sister, and was on her way to Norfolk. You may be sure that Matilda did not take her leave of John Sellers, for he was wise enough to keep well out of the way for fear his sister-in-law would divulge his guilty secret.

Matilda had spent a year working as a bank clerk in Holt. Richard's good friend, William Sayer, was a bank manager in that Norfolk town, and he had agreed to take Matilda on as his new ledger clerk. She had also been a lodger in his house, and she and Mrs M Sayer, his wife, had become friends. Mrs Sayer had signed herself with the initial "M" in Matilda's little purple birthday book, and no matter how much Matilda had cajoled her, M would not divulge her full name! So Matilda thought of a different name every day, and used to tease her friend unmercifully by calling her Marjorie, Magdalene, Millie, Marigold, Marianne, Margaret and May! But never Matilda!

In 1883 she had come back to *Waddington Terrace*, and had done the accounts ever since.

"What would I do without you?" Richard asked. This rhetorical question was no patronising compliment. It was meant from the bottom of his heart. She was his right hand, and his two business ventures had gone from strength to strength, with her there to guide and advise him.

Richard looked at Matilda as she sat there at her desk. The morning sunlight streamed in through the window, making her chestnut hair shine with unsurpassed brilliance. At forty-one, she was as beautiful now as she was when she entered his house for the very first time. He felt twenty years younger in her company – no, thirty years younger! However, in the mornings, when he looked in the mirror in his dressing-room and regarded his bald pate, his surround of white hair, and his white whiskers, the reality of the effects of the ravages of time brutally stared him back in the face.

Matilda honestly replied, "What would I ever have done without you?"

He had been her saviour in her time of need, he had understood when she had to go away to help her sister, he

176

had secured her employment in the bank, and she now enjoyed her present security.

Most of all, she loved him. Her heart-flutterings on that first day in *Waddington Terrace* had been the first stirrings of love, but she had to keep her feelings to herself. Now as she looked at him, she still admired what she saw: his broad shoulders, his upright body, his long tapering fingers, his kind brown eyes.

The door-bell rang. It was precisely ten o'clock and Mr Rogers, accompanied by his two clerks waited on the doorstep to be admitted. Richard walked down the length of the vestibule to the front door to do that service.

Normally the house-servant would open the door to visitors, but Alice Harrison, the reliable and tidy girl whom they had employed for five years had left to get married a week ago. Their new house-servant, who went by the name of Molly Reilly, had still not conformed to the usual dress codes of people in her line of work. Richard supposed it was because she was Irish, but perhaps it was because she was still very young. She had not learnt how to put her mop cap centrally on the top of her head, or how to tie back her black curly hair into some kind of order. She did not even know how to tie a neat, full bow at the back of her apron. And her skirt was tending towards this dreadful modern fashion of showing four inches of ankle. He would have to get his wife to take her in hand. As it was, Molly looked too much like a scarecrow to do the job of opening the door to his business colleagues or to his wife's lady-callers.

Joseph Rogers, a dapper little man in a black morning coat, wing-collared shirt, grey waistcoat, black satin cravat and pin-stripe trousers, took it all in his stride. He was a new solicitor in town, a replacement for Richard's old solicitor who had died, and was careful with his Ps and Qs, almost to the point of obsequiousness. He did not want to lose valuable custom by showing any personal feelings or critical thoughts. He would be circumspect and professional, no matter what befell. He followed Richard into the library, where the business of the morning was to be conducted.

The two clerks, Thomas Allpress and Samuel Rivett, had never been in a room which had so many books. Wearing identical dark suits and high, starched collars which all young men in this trade wore at this time, they stood open-mouthed at the doorway, before being offered a seat. On either side of the fireplace, there were two sizeable alcoves, shelved from top to bottom. There would have been well over four hundred books in each. They included the complete works of Shakespeare in five boxed sets: the histories, the comedies, the tragedies, the romances, and the sonnets. Each of these boxes was a collector's item and the whole set was a valuable asset. Some of Richard's old treasures from the *Vine House* nursery were here too: *The Arabian Nights*, *Treasure Island* and *Robinson Crusoe* among them. There were text books from his sons' days at the King's School Ely, some of Frances's books on philosophy and music, and their large family bible.

"Now," began Mr Rogers, "you want to make a new will. Am I right, that this is the purpose of the visit?"

"It's more an amendment and an addition."

"You mean a codicil?"

"Not really. Circumstances have changed. Some parts of my original will should remain the same and some parts of it need to be amended, and added to."

"Should we start, perhaps, with the new circumstances," suggested Mr Rogers, nodding to the two clerks to open up their writing-cases and prepare themselves to write all that he was about to dictate.

"Before we begin, I wish my wife to be present," said Richard as he pulled the bell-cord. He realised, too late, that he should have gone for his wife himself, to prevent Molly Reilly being paraded before the public eye. Molly appeared at the door, a scarecrow vision of wisps of hair, trailing apron tails, and ankles.

"You rang, sir?" she lisped in a pronounced Dublin brogue with its unmistakable retroflex R sound at the end of "sir". This was the first time she had met important visitors in the house. She looked scared to death of these important men who resembled three black birds or prey! A sort of role-reversal, for it was she who was fit to scare the crows!

She had, Richard noted, addressed him as "sir" and had dropped him a curtsy, and, although it was an awkward affair, it did show her to be willing.

"Would you ask my wife if she would be good enough to join me in the library!" commanded Richard, but he spoke kindly and slowly, so that Molly felt a little less frightened.

"Yes, sir." The poor girl escaped as quickly as she could.

A minute later, the door opened and in walked Matilda.

Mr Rogers stood up. He liked what he saw: Matilda's simple green dress with its high lace collar, the pleated bodice, the full flowing skirt: her chestnut hair which peeped from under a little lace cap. This must be the client's daughter? Or perhaps his secretarial assistant? He waited to be introduced.

"I don't believe you have met," said Richard. "My dear, this is Mr Rogers, my solicitor. Mr Rogers, may I introduce you to my wife."

Mr Rogers bowed to Matilda, and she inclined her head. Later he was to admit to some members of his club, held monthly at *The Lamb Hotel*, "You could have knocked me down with a feather!"

As Matilda sat at the little escritoire near the window, she was inwardly amused at his typical reaction. Everyone she met was surprised at how young she was. Many people took her for Richard's daughter, and addressed her as Miss Porter. Of course, she had been "Miss Porter" all of her life, so it was not as embarrassing for her as it was to the unfortunates who made the mistake!

The two clerks had been struggling to stand up: their employer had done so when Matilda entered, but what with their writing-cases open on their laps, their ink-bottles open, paper spread out on the leather-inlaid miniature desks and a quill pen in their right hands, it was almost an impossibility.

"Please, don't stand up," Matilda said, putting them out of their misery. Their faces showed gratitude: in all their personal commotion, and as they were both only aged twenty-one, they had not taken much notice of Matilda's youth. To them she looked the same age as their mothers: old!

To Richard's sons, however, she was young! Far too young! She was younger than they were, for God's sake!

How the comfortable worlds of these two men had been shattered in the January of 1884, when their widowed father announced that he was to be married to Matilda! The news was first broken to them in a most matter-of-fact communication:

"I am to marry my cousin's daughter, and am desirous of your blessing!"

Alfred had been appointed Head Brewer in the Leeds and Wakefield Brewery, and had settled to a comfortable family life with his wife Ellen and their two children, Basil and Cissie. Frank, who lived in Enfield, followed in his father's and brother's footsteps in the brewing business. He had not yet reached the dizzy heights of his older brother, and he had refused the offer of becoming head brewer for his father back in Ely, but he too lived a comfortable life with his wife Nina and their two children, Harold and Cecil.

Letters had been exchanged at an unprecedented rate between Alfred and Frank. They even met to discuss the matter.

"It is quite intolerable," Alfred voiced his thoughts. "Has our father taken leave of his senses?"

Frank was in agreement: "He clearly has forgotten where his duty lies. He has two sons and four grandchildren to consider!"

"We must unite on the matter of our inheritance."

180

"We must tell him that his intentions to marry Matilda are totally unacceptable."

"He must be brought round to our way of thinking."

"She is hardly a suitable wife: the daughter of that weak branch of the family."

"It seems quite immoral: he's old enough to be her father."

"He's a grandfather too… hardly a good example to the children."

"And she will outlive him. Then what happens to our inheritance?"

"And what if they have children?"

"God forbid!"

"She must be after his money!"

"I for one do not intend to see our inheritance and our children's entitlement frittered away by some gold-digger!"

Alfred and Frank had been united in their opposition to their father's remarriage. Alfred penned a letter, endorsed by Frank, to explain to their father their serious objections to this forthcoming fiasco.

We may note here that they showed little understanding of their father's last five years of sadness and loneliness since their mother's death in 1878, and there was an equal dearth of compassion for their distant relation, Matilda, whose circumstances had left her with next to nothing. Living so far away, and being so immersed in their own affairs, they had no knowledge of the part Matilda had lately played in their father's life, since she had come back to Ely: how hard she had worked, as Richard's book-keeper and house-keeper and companion, all rolled into one.

When Richard had received this letter from his sons, he was rightly incensed. How dare his sons dictate to him! They had taken little enough interest in his business or his welfare for many a year. He had always played fair by his sons with regard to equal inheritance, as he had promised he would all those years ago. They had always known they would own half the brewery each. And what is more they would inherit one hundred pounds apiece when he died in lieu of the *Vine House* brewery.

Frances had become more and more depressed after they had moved away from Ely and he blamed them for her untimely death.

It was Matilda who had helped him to develop the carrier business. Surely she had worked hard enough to deserve an equal share of his money! She had worked harder in the two businesses than either of his sons!

Together he and Matilda had sat in the library to draft a reply, in answer to all of Alfred's and Frank's misgivings, to allay their fears. There was, however, a flippant tone at the start of the letter which signified a dismissal of their objections, mixed with sarcasm.

Dear Alfred, I am very pleased with the letter you and Frank sent in answer to mine in respect of being married. There is not a word in it I object to.

"My dear, I think it would be better if you changed the *I* to *we*," said Matilda who was acting as secretary. "It would carry more weight. Two of us, and two of them, as it were!"

So the redrafted opening to the letter read:

Dear Alfred, we are very pleased with the letter you and Frank sent in answer to mine in respect of being married. There is not a word in it we object to.

"Knowing Miss P, as I do," dictated Richard, reverting immediately to the first person singular, *"I can say that she is an honourable woman."*

"Richard, my dear, I think a few more words of praise would not go amiss at this point," suggested Matilda. "Perhaps we should include *high-principled*?"

"Excellent, my dear, and also *conscientious and consistent*. Yes, that has a very nice ring to it. Will you write those in too?"

So the letter began to take shape:

I can say that she is an honourable, high-principled, conscientious and consistent woman, whose views and inclinations correspond with my own in a remarkable manner, and that we have every hope of being very happy with each other.

In answer to his sons' mercenary objections, Richard tried to mollify them on both counts of money and effects:

I propose to allow her an annuity should she be the longest liver of £40 per year, to invest £600 of my life insurance, with you and Frank as trustees, and £10 per year out of my other property for life, and after her decease to come to you and your children. Also to give her the furniture in the home absolutely, except two feather beds and the little silver which would come to you after her death.

On the question of any issue resulting from the marriage, Richard was more enigmatic: on the one hand, he had seemed to deny the possibility of any children, and on the other hand he vaguely alluded to providing for a child, should it be necessary:

Should there be any family, which I have no fear of whatever, some provision must be made.

Back to the financial arrangements for Matilda, he suggested the following:

"It won't cost any more to maintain her as a wife than it does now!" This line made Richard and Matilda both giggle like naughty children caught in the act, because of the immoral connotations, so it had to be scored out.

Instead he said: *"Should I be spared for some few years and the business goes on as it does now, I shall be able to make more money which she would have."*

All this talk of money had served to make Matilda acutely aware that because of her comparative poverty, Alfred and Frank might consider her to be a gold-digger, taking advantage of a rich man.

"Richard, I would like you to include this sentiment," and she had spoken out loud the words which she wrote in the following short paragraph:

"Miss P has no property or money, which she very much regrets."

It had then been Richard's turn to dictate, *"but I can say, she is a fortune in herself, and possesses such qualities which I value more than money."*

Matilda looked up at him from her little escritoire at which she was seated. She smiled at him, so openly full of love for him, that he was on the point of walking over to her and stroking her lustrous hair. He had to bring his mind back to less sensuous matters and refocus on the completion of this important letter.

He had to inform his sons how helpful Matilda had been in his haulage business. So he continued to dictate, and Matilda once more dipped her quill pen into the little reservoir containing black Indian ink, and wrote:

With regard to current proceeds in the business, what money I can make will go to pay off mortgages. I have paid off £200 this month to Mr Bailey, and we shall be very careful in making the best of everything, and Miss P is a great assistance to me in the business.

I have sent a copy of this letter to Frank and I hope both of you will write as soon as you can, for I wish to have it settled directly. I shall be glad to hear of anything you may suggest, for I wish to do everything for the benefit of all.

The final sentence was the pièce de résistance. There was no arguing with it: *I rather think we shall be married at Preston, at her sister's, and most likely you and Ellen, and Frank and Nina will be invited.*

Despite all of Richard's efforts, Alfred and Frank wrote numerous polite refusals to attend the wedding. They were angry, disappointed, and keenly felt the way they had been all but side-lined with the words, *most likely you will be invited*. Richard and Matilda had meant nothing more than the fact that they were as yet unsure of what format the wedding was to take. Alfred and Frank chose to think it an insult. They did not attend the wedding, which was held in Preston in June 1884. They had failed in their desperate attempt to dissuade their father: they would not be there to have the deed paraded in triumph before them.

Richard was saddened by all this: yet another family division! When would they ever end?

But some of the family had stuck together, and celebrated Richard's and Matilda's wedding with them.

Priscilla had been there. Not husband John, for he had run off to America to marry a younger woman, leaving Priscilla, like her mother before her, with a dismal future as a divorcee with four children.

Richard's sister Suzanna and her husband Edward Mann had gone up to Preston by train. They were going on to the Lake District afterwards for a summer holiday by Lake Windermere.

Richard's sister Ann was also there. She had always determined that hers was to be the celibate and lonely life of a spinster, but as she got older she had been able to delight in other people's weddings and honestly wish joy to the bride and groom.

Richard's brother Charles, who you may remember was a veterinary surgeon in Ely, and his wife Mary Moody had also attended. They had been Richard's closest friends and stalwart allies through the years, and they had helped Frances in her times of depression, especially when Alfred and Frank had moved away. Charles and Mary, who had celebrated their fortieth wedding anniversary two years before, were so happily married that they wished Richard happiness too in his declining years. They had warmly congratulated Matilda and wished her "happiness and wealth, and health to enjoy it".

And Richard's youngest brother, Henry John, the "love-child", went some way to making amends, by sending a telegram, which was read out to the assembled guests at the reception held in *The Station Hotel* in Preston. Richard had felt touched by the thought, and considered that time was perhaps the greatest healer, and that in time his sons would come round.

Mary and Rachel had sent their best wishes written on pink, scented paper, and Edna visited in early December with her husband Thomas, bringing with them two live turkeys "to be fattened up for Christmas"!

"Now, Mr Rogers," said Richard, "I want to confirm in writing all the provisions contained in an indenture made on the 16th June 1884, namely the settlement made to my present wife at the time of our marriage. You have a copy of that in your possession. Your late predecessor drew it up."

"Yes, of course, sir. I have it here with me." He patted his little black case as he spoke.

Richard stood up and from the mantelpiece he took down a framed picture.

"Now, for the main reason for your visit," he said, fondly holding the gilt frame.

"I don't understand," Mr Rogers was feeling perplexed. Was this a rare picture-frame to be valued and left in his will to some distant relation? He was at a loss, but his expression remained impassive and inscrutable.

Richard handed him the frame. Inside it was a sepia photograph of a little girl in a pretty white frock, a little girl with sparkling brown eyes and a head of blonde curls.

"She is a delightful little girl," Mr Rogers said simply and honestly, yet waiting for some explanation. He did not like guessing games and he had had enough surprises for one day.

"This is Ada Mary," Richard said, and Mr Rogers was none the wiser, but he nodded anyway.

"Ada is our daughter!" Matilda helped him out.

"Your daughter!" Mr Rogers repeated, doing his utmost to keep a dead-pan expression, so as not to show his initial surprise, then his incredulity, then realisation and acceptance, and finally admiration that a man of his client's age could actually father a child!

"I wish to make provision for her," said Richard.

"She is in the nursery at present with Miss Brand, her governess, engaged in learning how to read," said Matilda with pride. "She is a very advanced child for her age."

"As for the provision for Ada," continued Richard, "I wish to appoint my two sons and my friend Philip Allen as co-executors of this will."

Now, Alfred and Frank had happily agreed to be co-executors of their father's original will, made when their mother was still alive; they had begrudgingly agreed to be co-executors of their father's indenture giving Matilda a marriage settlement; but they were downright unhappy about the role they were to be forced to play with regard to their half-sister Ada, who was younger than most of their own children!

Handing Mr Rogers a sheet of paper, Richard was saying, "This gives the exact details of that provision, some £200 to be invested on her behalf, and used for her education, advancement and maintenance during her minority, and so on. Now when all that is written in your legalistic jargon, I shall sign my name to it."

Jimmy Stokes brought the Porter carriage round to the front of *Waddington Terrace*. He took great pride in this shining, royal-blue vehicle which sported the Porter crest on each side, and kept it in excellent order, polishing it with loving care once a week. His friend, Matthew, who considered himself to be something of a comedian, would call it a 'cart' or a 'wagon', but it was in fact a Victoria, named after their adored monarch. Queen Victoria's golden jubilee five years ago had popularised this particular model, which was a light-weight, low-slung carriage, easy to get in and out of. In the summer, the hood could be folded back for those balmy days when Richard, Matilda and Ada would go for a ride through the countryside around Ely.

Jimmy lifted Ada up into the carriage, treating her like a little lady. "There you are, Miss Porter. Now you make yourself nice and comfortable."

He thought how pretty she looked, in her pale blue dress and matching coat, and her little pill-box hat on her head, secured with a blue, satin ribbon tied in a bow at the side of her cheek. She sat there demurely with her little hands folded in her lap.

"Thank you, Mr Stokes," her musical voice chimed. Matilda had taught her to be polite to all manner of people, rich or poor, and it was an endearing quality, which won Ada affection, friendship and loyalty throughout her life.

Richard now sat beside his daughter.

"Well, Ada, this is an exciting day for you, is it not? Your very first visit to Ely market."

"Mother says I am to hold your hand all the time, and never let go, otherwise I might get lost." Ada looked apprehensively at him.

Richard could now hear his own mother's words ringing in his head. How scared he had been on his first visit to Ely market! How he had imagined all the terrible things that would befall him in Potter's Lane! Seventy years ago!

"You are not going to get lost, my lovely," he comforted her, patting her hands, and, taking his little girl's mind off her worries, he said, "Look there's Mother at the window! Wave goodbye to her!"

When they alighted from the Victoria, he took her hand in his, and together they walked up Market Place with its overhanging buildings. It was no longer a squalid street with slimy gullies, for the Public Health Acts and new sanitary inventions had led to cleaner streets with no risk of cholera anymore. Queen Victoria had been instrumental in effecting the Sanitary Reform Movement during the fifties, after her son, the Prince of Wales, had almost died of cholera. Since

188

then all new homes had been built with a water closet or ash-pit privy, and many homes had a water supply with brick sewers in place. Latterly Thomas Crapper had developed a new system to improve the "flushing loos", which had first been seen in the ladies rooms in the Crystal Palace during the Great Exhibition of 1851.

At the corner where Market Place gives way to Market Street, Richard heard himself say, like his father before him, "Good morning, Mr Kempton, how is business?" to the greengrocer who occupied that site, like his forebears. This was fast becoming a trip down memory lane!

To Ada he said, "Take note of Mr Kempton, Ada, for he is one of a rare breed of men. His family have been greengrocers on that very site since before the days of Oliver Cromwell. Truly amazing!"

When they turned the final corner into Ely Market, Ada stood stock still. "Father, look at all the people. There are hundreds and thousands and millions." Ada was just beginning to learn her figures, and had not yet mastered the art of being able to visualise large numbers with many noughts tacked on to the end.

You may suppose that she held on to her father's hand very tightly indeed when they made their way between the stalls. Richard noted his daughter's wide eyes dancing with delight one moment, as she listened to an old man who played a concertina, and with concern the next, as she regarded his chained monkey sitting balefully beside him.

"We shall give him a few pennies," Richard said to cheer his daughter, "to buy some monkey nuts."

"Father, may we go and see." Little Ada's dark brown eyes were dancing again, as she looked towards the butter market.

She raised her brown eyes to him so appealingly, and tugged his hand so encouragingly, that he was unable to resist her.

An excited crowd was standing round a platform on which a fortune-teller was seated. He felt inexplicably drawn towards her: there was a strange, déjà-vu inevitability about the whole affair. He could see Madame Zorra as clearly as if it were yesterday. He was to be disappointed, however, for this fortune-teller was different, not even really eastern or foreign. She had dark wavy hair, similar to Molly Reilly's untidy mop; her eyes were green, not brown and eastern; she had tied a pink muslin scarf round the crown of her head; she wore a cotton dress tie-dyed to look as if it had been made in India. With cheap, brass coins dangling round her forehead, a purple silk shawl edged with a straggly silver fringe, she looked to be playing a well-worn part, more like a cheap stereotype, thought Richard, than the real fortune-teller who had spoken to him in this spot when he was a boy.

He remembered that time long ago, when Madame Zorra had knelt down and taken his hand. The words she had uttered in that intimate moment had always been with him.

"I see a long life," she had said. Of course, she had said that to everyone, but he, Richard, had had a long life, with not a day's illness, and God willing he had many more years still to run.

"I see wives and children," she had said. He had not even considered the significance of "wives" at the time. But Madame Zorra had been right: first, his beloved Frances, with her gorgeous red hair and her ever gentle ways; and now Matilda, his serene and good wife, in whose eyes he saw love, and who had borne him his darling daughter. He had had five children, three still living. He thought about the two little sons who had not survived. What would they have said, he wondered, about his marriage to Matilda? Would they accept Ada less reluctantly as their sister than Alfred or Frank had done?

"I see family divisions," she had said. She had been right there, over and over again: his father and Uncle William, Uncle William and Marshall, Ann and Marshall, Marshall and himself, Henry John and himself, Alfred and Frank and himself, and "up north" even Priscilla and John had recently got divorced!

"I see a full circle," she had said. He still did not know what that meant, but it had been strange that the other fortune-teller at the Haddenham Holiday Fair had said exactly the same thing.

She had been right too in her other prediction, as it turned out. Her words had seemed odd at the time, but they had eventually made sense: "You will lose what your heart desires, but your heart will desire what you choose."

He had lost Ann, but his strong desire for Frances had been overpowering, and, although in choosing Matilda, he had not thought to have any children by her, he had found himself physically drawn to her, she who was the daughter of the one he had lost.

"Would you be wanting the little girl's fortune told?" this present apology for a fortune-teller asked Richard.

He heard the unmistakable retroflexed sounds in her pronunciation of "girl" and "fortune" and was about to move on. An Irish tinker was what she was, he decided!

"Go on, sir, give your granddaughter a treat!"

He found himself mechanically contradicting her assumption that he was Ada's grandfather. He forgave everyone who made the mistake, for he was old enough to be her grandfather. His cousin Marshall, once his friend, was her real grandfather.

"Oh, Papa, please," Ada begged.

"Just a silver sixpence, sir. It won't break the bank!" the fortune-teller was edging him to give in.

"On one condition," he said.

"Ooh!" a woman beside him crooned to her friend Sadie. "I likes a man who makes conditions. It's so masterful, I always says!"

"Ssh!" Sadie said, "Let's hear it!"

"Ask away," the fortune-teller sat back and folded her arms. This was the kind of customer she could well do without. Times had been hard enough for her since landing in Liverpool from Dublin's not so fair city, and the sooner she got rid of this old man the better. Siobhan, for that was her name, pursed her lips in an unattractive pout of belligerence.

"In your profession," Richard said, politely enough, "what is meant by 'a full circle'?"

Now Siobhan suddenly unfolded her arms and looked with interest at the old man.

"Where did you hear that?" she asked.

"What's a full circle?" Sadie asked.

"How would I know?" replied her friend. "You shushed me, so now you listen to what she says and we'll find out."

Richard was not going to divulge all the secrets of his past to the people standing around, so he simply asked, "What does it mean? Do you know?"

"Yes, I know," she answered, now sitting forward to speak to him, aware of the drama she was making of the situation and of the stir in her audience which might result in a few sixpences coming her way.

Siobhan spread both arms wide, with her palms upturned, before Ada. "Here is your full circle! Your little girl!" was all she said, and then she took Ada's hand.

Ada was suddenly scared. She did not like this woman at all now, and she pulled her hand away.

"Thank you," said Richard and gave a shilling to this fortune-teller, who perhaps was not such a charlatan after all.

As this old man was being led by the fair-haired child to some other part of the market, Siobhan called after him, at her unexpected good fortune,

"God bless you, sir!"

She set about making money from the next batch of gullible people.

After dinner, Richard and Matilda were sitting in the library. Normally, they would retire to the drawing room, or as Richard's grandfather would have chuckled and said, "Or is it withdraw to the retiring room?", but this evening was different.

"I have a few things I wish to write, Richard, before the day is over," Matilda had said earnestly.

"Then let us retire to the library. You can sit by the window. There's still enough light in the sky for you to see what you are doing."

Richard was content to sit in the library of an evening. It was his favourite room, as he was always among friends with his books. Tonight he had selected *The Tempest* and had taken it out of its box of similar Shakespeare plays. The red leather-bound volume was open, propped up on his brass book-rest, which was placed across the arms of his leather armchair. It was a mistake, Richard decided within a few minutes, to have selected this sombre play. On turning the pages near the end of Act Five, he read old Prospero's words, "Every third thought shall be my grave".

It set Richard's mind thinking. For two hours of today, when he had re-written his will making provision for those whom he loved and would miss, those words might have applied to him; but, in normal circumstances, Richard lived for the morrow. Shakespeare must have had a pessimistic view of old age, he thought, but then, what did he know? He never reached it, dying at the age of fifty-two!

Richard looked out at the clear evening sky, the promise of halcyon days to come, and the thought of country rides in the Victoria with Matilda and Ada, or journeys by train to Cambridge, and perhaps even a visit to London to see the River Thames, Big Ben and the Houses of Parliament. They would visit Priscilla in Preston, to introduce Ada to her cousins. They would ask Alfred and Frank for a weekend's visit: Alfred's daughters, Edith and Ethel, and Frank's daughter, Elsie, would be fine playmates for Ada. Time to patch up old quarrels.

He got up to choose a book more in accord with his optimism and zest for life. He may be seventy-six, but he had everything to live for.

"I live for my little girl," Matilda was writing to her friend M in Holt. She had begun the letter: "My dear Mab" delighting in her choice of name beginning with M for her friend, for Mab was the queen of the fairies, the bringer of dreams, the one who could make dreams come true. Matilda was going to ask a big favour of her friend.

"What is it you write?" asked Richard.

"I am writing a letter to M. I am trying to ascertain whether or not she and William, would be able to look after Ada, should the eventuality occur."

"What eventuality, my dear?"

"Her being left an orphan, as a minor."

Richard laughed. "Matilda, it is all this last will and testament talk today. It has gone to your head. It is hardly a likely eventuality!"

"But it might happen!"

"Nonsense!" said Richard with conviction. Yes, he himself may well die before Ada reached the age of twenty-one, but not Matilda. "I think it would be better not to write that to M, my dear, for it may give her unnecessary cause for alarm!"

So, instead, Matilda praised Ada's accomplishments and told of how well she was progressing under the care of Miss Brand the governess. She wrote the doting mother's minutiae of how Ada had been tucked up in bed that very evening and how Ada had fallen asleep as she was reading her the story of *Sleeping Beauty*. It was a lovely letter for its simplicity, ending: "for indeed, she is our own precious sleeping beauty, and I am sure one day she will meet her handsome prince, and live happily ever after." It was a letter which M was to fondly reread for many a year.

Some time later, just before the light disappeared from the sky, Richard reached for the bell-pull and rang for Mollie to light the oil lamps, and to bring in the port decanter and two glasses on a silver salver. After she had performed these two duties and had left the room, he said to Matilda,

"You will have to take that girl in hand. She needs a mother's care! I don't think she has any notion of the meaning of the word 'tidy'."

"She is a poor, unfortunate, young girl, Richard. But we will make something of her. I will start tomorrow morning with a hairbrush!"

Richard went back to his reading, but this time he started to reread *Treasure Island*. This story of a young boy's dreams coming true was one which he knew he would enjoy. It suited his frame of mind, for he was relieved after all that had happened during the day: the writing of the new will, the fortune-teller's answer to his question, Matilda's improvement after her fall.

Matilda sipped her port, enjoying the soft but fiery sweetness as it trickled down her throat. It made her want to cough, but she breathed deeply and waited till the spasm abated. Thoughtful now, she took out one of her silver-edged, printed visiting cards from the little drawer in the escritoire. On the one side in silver copperplate writing was her name, *Mrs Richard Porter*. She took up her pen, and, on the other side of the card, she wrote a few words.

Then from the same drawer she took out her mother's little black purse. She did not use it any more, for it had been showing the signs of wear and tear. It was the only reminder which she had of her mother. It was one of Matilda's most cherished possessions: indeed, it was her only real personal possession. Inside the stamp-pocket was the Penny Black, so dog-eared now that it would never be an heirloom! In the middle section of the purse there was a folded piece of paper containing a few jokes written by her sister Ada. Tucked inside the compartment with the press-stud flap there was a small flat package, wrapped in fine white paper, addressed to "Ada Porter". Into the front compartment Matilda placed the visiting card.

"What is it you do?" asked Richard, becoming aware that she was fiddling with something.

Matilda looked at him so seriously that he closed his book.

"I have been thinking how good you have been to me, Richard."

"But you look so serious, my dear. I am sure you have no need to think that my being good to you is the end of the world! You have been good to me, and see, I am smiling!"

"Today, with Mr Rogers here, has made me realise that I have so little, so little to bequeath."

Richard interrupted her with a sighing, "Matilda! You really must not let today's events trouble you."

Matilda was undeterred. There was something important she had to say. "I would like you to make me a promise," she said.

"A promise? Of course, my dear. What is it?"

"If I die before you do…"

Richard was about to say something, but Matilda raised her hand to be heard. "If I die before you do," she continued, "I would like you to give this little purse to Ada. It is the one possession that is truly mine. I should like her to have it when I die. Will you promise me you will do this for me?"

"If it will make you happy, of course I will promise," he said. There was no point in pursuing earlier lines of discussion, as this promise clearly meant so much to Matilda. To reassure her he said again, "I promise."

He smiled.

She was beautiful, thought Richard. Life had been good to him.

She smiled.

Matilda was relieved, her mind had been put at rest: but, deep down, her heart went out to her Richard. There he sat, oblivious of the ugly truth as yet.

That afternoon she had had a violent fit of coughing, and had coughed up blood.

Chapter 9

RICHARD

1st December 1892

In the morning, when the rest of the house was quiet, before
Ada was awake, and before all the people were due to arrive
at his house, Richard opened the little drawer in Matilda's
escritoire and took out her purple birthday book. Today was
Matilda's birthday. He sat on her chair and, by the light
which filtered in through the chink in the drawn curtains, he
gently turned the pages of the year and read the entries.

On January 19th, Matilda had written his name, for that
was his birthday. Now, he was nearly seventy-seven years
old. It was a sobering thought for a man with a five-year-old
daughter!

On February 10th, he saw she had recorded the death of
her mother, Ann. Dear Ann! Richard's thoughts were
confused as the images of Matilda and Ann seemed to roll
into one. The chestnut hair, the ivory skin, the blue eyes, the
endearing smile.

On March 23rd, Matilda had written the birthday of Mary
Moody. What a great source of strength she and Charles had
always been. They had been so good to Frances; they had
been so kind to Matilda. He hoped they would live to see
their golden wedding: they were good people who deserved
such a reward.

Marshall's sister Edna had signed her name too. "Ednor
Jones" was how she had signed her name, on July 4th her
birthday, favouring the more unusual spelling of her name.

Then there was the entry made on July 10th, the day that
Matilda's sister Ada had died. Ada had been named after her.

Ada's birthday, on July 20th, was recorded in Matilda's own characteristic version of sprawling copperplate writing. Richard's grandson, Harold Leslie's name was there too, for he shared the same birthday as Ada!

Alfred and Frank and their families' birthdays were all recorded in this little book. Matilda had done wonders in trying to bring the family together again.

Priscilla's wedding on August 6th was remembered too, and even the birthday of her wayward husband John Sellers. Their four children's birthdays were also included, as well as the date of death of two of them, ten-year-old Jessie and six-year-old Ida who had died within twenty-four hours of each other at the end of March in 1887.

Knight had also signed his name in November, but he decided to put his first name, William, the name he now preferred to be called, in memory of his father.

Matilda's friend M Sayer's birthday on December 22nd was entered too, a reminder to Richard of a letter he must now write, and a codicil he must add to his will.

Today was 1st December, Matilda's birthday, and on that page she had written her own name Matilda Ann Porter, the name she had always had and never had to change. Opposite was the little verse:

Ah! Whither could we flee for aid,
When tempted, desolate, dismay'd?
Or how each mighty foe defeat,
Had suffering saints no mercy seat?

Where were the *saints* now? Where had their merciful help been hiding, when Matilda needed their aid to defeat the mighty foe?

Richard dipped his pen in the well of ink and wrote the date "1892" beside her name on this, her birthday. This was the final entry in Matilda's little book, for this was the day she had died.

Ada looked at her mother, lying so peacefully and palely in bed, laid out with her hands crossed below her neck.

"Put them gently in her hands," Richard said. He and Ada had been out in the garden at the back of the house, the walled garden which Matilda had loved so much, in search of the first snowdrops. They had found just five.

"A snowdrop for every year of your life," he said.

Ada very solemnly put the precious, delicate flowers in her mother's hands. She was to remember this moment for the rest of her life!

"Her hands are cold, Papa," she said, bewildered, as tears began to well up in her eyes.

"Don't cry, my darling," he said. "We don't want to make Mama unhappy. She used to love little snowdrops. Do you know what she used to call them?"

Ada shook her head. The tears rolled down her cheeks.

"She said that snowdrops are nature's teardrops. And when they dry, the spring flowers will bloom and we will all be happy again."

He dabbed Ada's eyes with his handkerchief, as he led her away.

"I have something downstairs to show you, my dear," he said, and together they entered the library and went over to Matilda's escritoire. He opened the drawer and brought out the little black purse. "Come and sit on my knee. I made a promise to your mother before she died. This little purse was her own very special possession," he said. "She wanted you to have this, as your very own. Something to remember her by. I promised her that I would give it to you."

"Thank you, Papa," said Ada, holding the treasured item in her hands.

"Open it," he coaxed.

She opened the flap and inside she found the compartment fastened with a little press-stud. Inside was a paper package addressed to her.

"This is for me," she said. "May I open it?"

"Of course, my dearest, it is yours."

Ada opened the little package, a piece of paper folded about a lock of Matilda's chestnut hair.

Richard was too shaken to speak. The reddish brilliance of the lock of hair brought back so many memories: Matilda, Ann and Frances, all now united as one in death.

"It's so soft," Ada said and wrapped it up again.

Then she took out the card with silver edging. On the one side were written the words *Mrs Richard Porter*, all in silver copperplate, and on the other side was her mother's distinctive writing.

My dear little girl.
Oh my child, I shall soon have to leave you.
And when this is given to you, you will be a big girl.
This purse was given to my dear mother and now I give it to you.

In the quiet of the library on that dreary December morning, Richard put his arms round his daughter and rocked her to and fro.

"Soon we shall be able to go skating on the ice. You would like that, wouldn't you? And in the spring we shall go by train to Preston and visit your aunt Priscilla and your two cousins. And we'll visit Edith and Ethel and Elsie. That will be fun."

"And we can drive in the Victoria," Ada added.

"And in the summer we'll have picnics."

"And walks in the park."

"And trips to London."

"Shall we go to the fair?"

'The Porter Legacy': A Trilogy

Oh My Child is the first in this trilogy, followed by
Snowdrops for Ada and *Red Scar*.

Set in Ely and Preston and based on actual characters this
trilogy traces the changing fortunes and divisions within one
family during the nineteenth and early twentieth centuries.
Each book can be read separately; they tell independent
stories.

In the early morning on the first day of
spring, in the year of 1893, Ada was a
shivering bundle of excitement. This
was the day she had been looking
forward to. She was tired of wearing her
black taffeta mourning dress with its
little detachable and detestable, prickly
lace collar. She longed to wear her pink
brocade dress again with its long white
sash and its twenty-two shiny, satin
buttons down the front of the trim
bodice. She was only five years old, after all.

It was ever so cold in her bedroom, and the bedclothes
were ever so cosy, but neither of these would deter her from
getting out of bed and tiptoeing to the curtained sash
window. She pulled back the mint-green, velvet drapes to
look down on to the walled garden below, her very own
secret garden, with its fragile and fading memories. But
where she expected to see a host of yellow and purple
crocuses under the beech tree, she saw instead an
impenetrable blanket of snow, a bleak and hostile white
landscape.

Red Scar

Virginia
Aitken

Even yet, almost one hundred years on, under the old copper beech tree, and half obscured among dense undergrowth in a long forgotten corner, their wooden garden seat is still here. This is where they once sat together in the moonlight, dreamily looking out across the silvery camomile lawn to a life full of promise.

The once sweeping carriageway to *Red Scar* mansion is now overgrown, and fragments of the sandstone gateposts lie in a tangle of bindweed and ageing brambles at the further end of the estate. There is another gateway today, signposted, directing visitors to follow one-way traffic routes through rows of regimented trees, metallic benches and marble slabs. On one of the cold, vandal-proof benches you can just make out a memorial inscription on a blackening brass plate: "In Memory of Harry and Ada who loved this place".

This is their story.